I0536239

THE WINGED MEN

ALSO BY GARY LOVISI

Driving Hell's Highway

Gargoyle Nights: A Collection of Horror

Mars Needs Books!: A Science Fiction Novel

*Murder of a Bookman: A Bentley Hollow
Collectibles Mystery Novel*

Violence Is the Only Solution

As Editor:

Battling Boxing Stories

*The Great Detective: His Further Adventures:
A Sherlock Holmes Anthology*

THE WINGED MEN

The Jon Kirk of Ares Chronicles: Book 1

GARY LOVISI

A Scientific Romance inspired by Edgar Rice Burroughs'
John Carter Series and set upon the faraway planet Ares

WILDSIDE PRESS

This novel was originally published as *The Winged-Men* by Fading Shadows Press in book form in 1997 in a small limited edition. This new version has been substantially rewritten and revised for this new edition.

Published by Wildside Press LLC.
www.wildsidebooks.com

NAMES OF PEOPLE AND PLACES APPEARING IN THE JON KIRK CHRONICLES

ANDU; a great warrior and friend to Jon Kirk.

ARES: the planet under the red sun in the Orion System that Earthman Jon Kirk finds himself transported to.

ARESANS: the human-like peoples who are the inhabitants of the planet Ares and the eastern continent of Cos. Many of the men are green skinned with dark hair, while the women are lighter in color and have red or green hair.

ARMEN; King of the Sar Nomads, friend of Jon Kirk.

CALAIT: name of the old Zaran city that was renamed Tarcos.

CHAVAS: a rat-like creature, also it is a high insult to be called a chavas.

CORON: a farmer.

COS: the eastern continent of the planet Ares inhabited by the green human-like race and the Zaran winged-men.

CROOCH: a Southern Farmer and a vile traitor.

DAMETON: the brother of Tazo, from the Southern Farmer Caste and a friend to Jon Kirk.

DARG: called "king" of prisoners in the cells before the Games of Zar.

GOPON: Zaran, overseer of female slaves in the palace of the King of Caliat.

HOAM: an Ares green man general, defeated by the Winged-men in the distant past, known today as Hoam the Hero, and the direct ancestor of the treacherous King Tob.

JON KIRK: Adventurous Earthman and heroic soldier transported to the planet Ares.

MANALIA: Zaor's mate, fire-red haired women.

OGZ: one of the Vaki Nomads, a mighty rival to Armen and his tribe.

ORLAZ: a madman held prisoner in the cells under the Arena.

ORTON: Zaran prince, new ruler of Caliat after his father, Pondonan is killed by Jon Kirk. He was later also killed by Jon Kirk.

PONDONAN: Zaran ruler of Caliat, killed by Jon Kirk. He was the father of Orton, who succeeded him, also killed by Jon Kirk.

POURK: a large reptilian animal used much in the same way as a horse is upon the Earth on the planet Ares. They are very fast moving beasts.

SAHN JOR: King of the Caste of Woodworkers who becomes a mighty warrior.

SALIAD: Zaran, the third and last Zaran King of Caliat before the city is conquered. He is also killed by Jon Kirk in battle.

SIRAH: the green-haired beauty who would become the mate of Earthman, Jon Kirk.

SAOK: a friend to Jon Kirk and Zaor.

TARCOS: formerly the Zaran city of Caliat, renamed in honor of Tar-Gool when it was conquered by Jon Kirk.

TAR-GOOL: an old green man, patriot and great scientist whose mission was to free his people from the Winged-men, the city Tarcos was later named in his honor.

TAVAN: a Southern Farmer.

TOB. king of the Warrior Caste traitor and enemy of Jon Kirk.

VAKON: a Southern Farmer, in league with the vile Crooch.

VOGNAR: the mythical unknown western continent of the planet Ares.

ZARANS: the name the Winged-men call themselves. They came to Ares ages ago in spaceships from the planet Zar and conquered the planet and its native human-like green hued people.

ZAOR: a young green warrior that Jon Kirk meets when in comes to Ares who befriends the Earthman, and the brother of Sirah.

CHAPTER 1

JON KIRK COMES TO ARES

The strange story I am about to relate to you will probably not be believed. This is up to you. You may see it as but the mad ravings of a deranged mind. If such is your opinion, then you are welcome to it. However, I think that it is an exciting narrative of a lone Earthman's adventures on a strange and alien world.

It was told to me by Jon Kirk, an old college friend of who having dropped out of school in 1967 enlisted in the U.S. Army and after boot camp was stationed in a place called Vietnam that few of us had heard of back then. He fought bravely for two years and proved a natural soldier and eventually was promoted to the rank of sergeant. As a sergeant, he was stationed in the northern city of Hue in South Vietnam during some of the heaviest fighting of the Tet Offensive in 1968.

Upon one of my frequent visits to his home to see his sister, my future wife, Janet, a letter from the United States Defense Department suddenly arrived. It was ominous, for I found Janet, her younger brother Stu, and her parents were all in a state of shock. When I asked what had happened, the parents only broke down and cried. Then Janet handed me the letter and I read it.

United States Defense Department
Washington. D.C.
April 28, 1968

Dear Mr. and Mrs. Kirk,
We regret to inform you that your son, Sergeant Jon Kirk, has been reported Missing In Action on or before February 1, 1968. We are sorry to report that he is presumed dead.
Sincerely,
General H.T. Tomnson
United States Army

It was terrible news. We did not want to believe the worst, and we tried to hang onto hope, but a few weeks later we were informed that Jon's body had been discovered. Eventually it was shipped home to the family and buried in a family plot at Green Acre Cemetery.

One would think that was the end of the story of Jon Kirk. As it would turn out, it was only the beginning.

* * * *

Years later, the past intruded into my calm and orderly world one day and this whole strange tale began. It had been years since Jon Kirk's death, and I had all but forgotten about him and moved on, but then with a ring of my doorbell—and as I answered the door—*there he was!*

Jon Kirk stood there right there in front of me when I opened the door!

"Jon!"

My mind raced, I almost fainted. The man I saw before me had been dead and buried for many years. Yet here he was, standing right there in front of me! I just stood by in open-mouthed shock and awe.

"Well, aren't you going to invite me in?" Jon Kirk asked me with that same warm smile I'd known from him for so many years, "Or aren't we still friends?"

"What? Of course, but…how?" I stuttered, hardly knowing what to say. I felt like I had seen a ghost. I guess, in some ways, I had!

He smiled at me, that same warm glowing smile, the Jon Kirk I had known for so long and loved as a brother. The good friend I had missed for so many years. Now he was here! There was no doubt in my mind that it had to be him. But how?

I grabbed his hand and shook it heartily.

"You're alive!" I shouted, fearful of what my eyes told me and of what he might say to me.

Jon Kirk just laughed lightly in his usual manner, "Of course I am alive."

He looked the same to me now just as he had looked before he had left for Vietnam so many years before. Tall, lean, well-built and muscled, with his raven black hair and those sharp steel-gray eyes. He was the same Jon Kirk I had always known.

"I can't believe it is you! You have to tell me what the hell happened!" I asked, unable to restrain my words and excitement any longer, feeling as if I had somehow gone mad, standing there talking to a man I knew to be dead and buried! "Jon, what happened?"

"It's a long story, my friend," he said, coming into my house and sitting down. He asked for a drink, and as we sat down while drinking more than a few beers that long June afternoon, this is the story I have written down in Jon Kirk's own words just as he told it to me that warm Summer day.

"As you know," Jon began "I was killed in the Vietnam War. Killed quite dead—and yet perhaps—not so dead as one might believe. It happened like this. My unit was in a firefight during Tet in the battle for Hue up in the northern part of South Vietnam. I got separated from my unit. I later found out that all the other men were killed. As it turned out, I was killed, too."

I gulped hard at that ominous admission.

He just smiled.

"Killed?" I asked, totally confused, fearing some joke or strange extenuating circumstance. "There must be some mistake?"

"It was no mistake. I was killed in battle. I was dead."

"Then… Then you were killed? Truly dead? But how can that be? How can you be here? If what you say is true—then you have risen from the grave!"

"Well yes, that is essentially true, but…" Jon admitted with a grim smile, noting my wonderment and incredulity. He went on to explain, "We were on patrol outside Hue, the northern provincial capital, and a key city, the focus of the North Vietnamese and Vietcong invasion of the South during the Tet Offensive. You may have read about it? It was big. Nasty. Bloody and bad."

I nodded as I looked at my friend. I recalled the battle in the news. It had been a turning point in the war on many levels, but this—? I looked at my friend closely. He was surely of flesh and blood, just like me, for had I not felt and shook his hand? It was warm, a warm-blooded hand. Yet he had been dead and buried. I had seen his body buried, and by his own admission he says he had been killed. Dead. I was thoroughly convinced I had finally lost my mind just then. Perhaps he was some kind of illusion? I even told him so.

"No, no my friend." Jon Kirk laughed, with that calm good humor of his, those steel-gray eyes of his shining with the power of life. "It's all true, but you see, while I am dead and buried on this world—on the planet Ares I have been alive and well for many years!"

I needed some time to digest these words. The planet...Ares? Two worlds? Simultaneous life existence? It seemed incredible!

Jon Kirk saw my obvious bafflement and continued, "I cannot explain it, but no sooner was I dead here on Earth, than I awoke upon the planet Ares, completely alive and well. I awoke a strong flesh and blood man again and in perfect health. Of course, at that time, I knew absolutely nothing of what had actually occurred or why. So I will tell it to you all now, just as it happened and eventually it will all become clear to you, as it did to me."

I could only nod blankly. Astonished but not wanting him to stop telling me his strange tale. I was fascinated by it and eagerly wanted to hear all he had to tell me.

"It happened like this. I awoke on Ares alone, terrified, and disoriented," Jon Kirk told me in simple clipped words. He laughed a bit, said, "You know, I thought I was either dead or mad. Certainly I had to be mad, or dreaming, or perhaps in Heaven. Though more likely, probably in Hell. I could not tell which. Instead where I found myself, was upon the planet Ares. A new world! Ares turned out to be a combination of a lot of things I have always yearned for in my life, all wound up in a wild world full of the kind of action and adventure I have always craved."

"Where is this...Ares?" I asked, eagerly, trying to get answers to stem my confusion and assuage my curiosity.

"To answer some of your questions, my friend, Ares, is a planet about 150 light years away from Earth, the fourth planet in the Orion system," he answered.

I nodded, though this meant very little to me at the time.

He smiled at me indulgently.

Well, of course, after that, I asked him a hundred more questions, unable to contain myself, and he just laughed and smiled good-naturedly. He was a patient man.

"Are you real? I mean are you actually alive here before me now?" I had to ask him.

"As to those questions, of course I am alive, but I am not physically there in your presence. What you see before you now is an energy field formed in my likeness. A great scientist named Tar-Gool from the planet Ares has invented a transmitter that can send me to you in this fashion. Or my image, I should say. Form with substance, you can feel the flesh on my bones, feel the warmth of that flesh, the blood in my veins, but it is not real. Though it does feel real to you. At this moment I am in Tar-Gool's laboratory light-years away from Earth, but my likeness is sitting across from you speaking as if I were right there with you. A neat trick, eh? To all intents and purposes the energy image is an exact likeness of me. It can speak, it has substance, you felt that when you shook my hand."

"It seems nothing short of…supernatural," I gasped.

"Super science, my friend," Jon Kirk corrected.

I nodded. "Extraordinary!"

"Indeed," he smiled broadly. "There is much that is extraordinary on Ares."

"I wish to hear all about it," I said. *"Everything!"*

Jon Kirk laughed deeply, "Well, my friend, that is why I am here. So why don't you crack open another beer, sit back, open your mind, and I will tell you the strange story of how I came to the world of Ares and what I beheld there."

CHAPTER 2

IN THE COASTAL MOUNTAINS

It s a terrible experience to die. I know, for I have done it, as must each one of us will do before we shuffle off this mortal coil. However a much more horrifying experience than dying, is that of waking from death!

When I awoke upon Ares, once more alive and healthy, I was laying upon my back stunned and scared. I found myself staring overhead at a deep blood red sky and a blood red sun with trembling fear. What could this be? Nothing here seemed right to me. It was the first time I can remember ever being so scared. I had always expected death, such is the companion of all fighting men everywhere, and was I not a soldier? Yet I never expected this!

A red sky! A blood-red sun! what was this? I thought I must dead and that I must be in Hell. I thought I had lost my sanity. However, I soon came to grips with myself, realizing that rather than fearing the unknown this new world presented to me, it was actually all rather intriguing. It was an incredible puzzle. It was a new challenge. I wondered just what was going on here, and I endeavored to find out.

I realized immediately one good result of this event, I was no longer wounded. I was not bleeding, nor in any pain, even though I had been shot in the head and had instantly been killed in that battle in Vietnam. And I *had* died! But *now* I was not dead! Neat trick, I thought. I wondered how I had done it.

There was something else. I was still in my U.S. Army uniform, still wearing my military boots. It was most unusual.

I moved my arms and legs, and everything seemed in splendid working order. I could feel a warm welcome breeze rustle my hair and blow against my cheek as it flowed past me. I was alive! I did not know how I had done it, but I was alive!

I stilled lived!

And I have always believed that where there is life, there is always hope.

I stood up, a little dizzy at first, and then took notice of my surroundings. They were certainly strange and wonderful, and I began to wonder again if I might be crazy or just dreaming? Maybe I really was dead and this was Heaven? It all seemed so strange, so fantastic. However, upon reflecting upon my Earthly life, I realized that I could just as well be in the 'other' place, down in Hell. I soon laughed it all off, and decided to take a look around at this new and most interesting environment.

I found myself on a small green sward-covered knoll, and all around me as far as I could see were endless plains with huge faraway mountains that soared into the blood red sky. Yes, it was certainly a red sky! Now I knew for sure that I wasn't in Kansas anymore as they say—which meant I was not anywhere on Earth either. An interesting predicament. I wondered, then, just where I might be?

I was trying to figure this all out as best I could when suddenly from behind me I heard footsteps approaching at a run. They were immediately followed by what seemed to be light-hearted girlish laughter, of all things. I looked up and was surprised to see two young women running rapidly towards me. They were laughing and screaming and constantly looked back behind them as if they were being chased.

One of the women had fire-red hair and the other had bright green hair. The green-haired girl surely caught my eye. I had never seen anyone like her before. I had never seen any woman that was so stunningly beautiful in all my life.

I noted that both women were young and extremely beautiful. One had long red hair and a lighter green-tinted skin. *Green skin!* That was certainly unusual. The other woman had a very light hue of green skin, but this time her hair was bright green, as were her eyebrows and full luscious lips. Her bright green hair hung in long straight locks. She was stunning. I found myself entranced by her beauty. Each woman wore slick black furs that offered only a skimpy covering, while the rest of their supple and amply-endowed bodies were adorned with all manner of glittering barbaric jewelry.

They still laughed as they ran closer to where I lay hidden watching them, still unnoticed by them. They looked back, shouted, and then turned forward and saw me for the first time. I must have presented quite the shock. Their laughter immediately stopped. They both stared at me for a moment startled, then they began screaming in terror.

I raised my hands in a peaceful gesture, certainly not intending them any harm, but hardly knowing how else to react or what to say. It did not matter anyway, for they could not understand my words, nor I theirs.

Then from a massive boulder behind them, a large clean-faced man suddenly jumped down into the clearing before us. He was green-skinned also, with dark hair and sharp eyes. He appeared to be a warrior of some kind and was heavily armed and armored in some type of chain mail. He caught the redheaded girl and laughing, threw her gently to the soft grass. She screamed, and pointed in terror over his shoulder. The man shot a glance up at me and in surprise quickly drew his sword from its scabbard. It seemed to be a Roman-type short sword, and the man walked slowly and carefully towards me uttering strange sounds in a language I could not understand. He eyed me warily, then continued his words more earnestly. More seriously and dangerously.

I shook my head indicating to him that I did not understand his words.

He did not seem to like that very much.

The two girls now positioned themselves behind the warrior in evident fear of me, for I could see they saw him as their protector. Well, I'll tell you, while they were all scared of me, I was just as scared of them. Curious too, mostly. I was out there all alone and seemingly helpless. My valued M-16 was not with me, probably having fallen to the jungle floor in far away Vietnam when I had been yanked out of there to here. Wherever *here* might be.

Instinctively, my hand went for my sidearm. I was relieved to feel the cold steel of my .45 still in its holster at my side. It was ready. So was I. I moved my other hand to feel for my bayonet slung down where I kept it, the hilt protruding from the top of my right boot.

I withdrew the bayonet and held it reassuringly in my right hand. It was almost as long as the warrior's short sword.

I spoke to the warrior, but obviously he could not understand me either. I tried again in every language I knew. It was all met with the same confusion and frustration on both our parts. Nevertheless, the warrior approached me carefully and in what looked now like a peaceful manner. The red-headed girl had already left the clearing, for the warrior had spoken some words to her that caused her to run off. To where, I could not guess. The other girl with the bright green hair stood by as if frozen looking at me intently, apparently unable to move. I stood by, frozen too, as the warrior slowly advanced.

We eyed each other warily. One soldier, or warrior, to another.

Then with a sudden, wild howl the warrior lunged forward in a mad rush upon me. Instantly I found myself in a deadly duel for my life. Our battle had begun.

Now, I had had some fencing experience in college, and in fact I had won numerous championships. I was accounted one of the best swordsmen in my class, and I knew that training and experience would come in very handy now. I hoped so, at least. However, I also knew that none of that training had been in actual warfare, it was all just a game. This was real. Nor had that been in a fight to the death, as this battle apparently was. However, I have always believed that necessity is the mother of invention and so I was determined to put up as good a defense as I was able. As it would turn out my swordsmanship wasn't half bad.

Immediately I parried the warrior's bold thrusts, one after the other his blows were deflected, though occasionally he would get through my guard and nick me, drawing some small amount of blood. He was persistent and an able swordsman. As the battle progressed, these nicks began to happen more and more so that after some time my body was covered with tiny crimson rivulets. It was a hard fought battle. My fencing was rusty, but I was recalling it all very quickly. In this fight you defended yourself from your enemy's blade, or you died. I put all I knew now to good use.

As the fight progressed I realized that my success so far had become a mere inconvenience to this highly trained swordsman. Try as I might, I knew that sooner or later he would win this contest. I knew too, that I had to do something fast to save myself from the wrath of his furious attacks. And as if the warrior could sense my apprehension in this regard he pressed his attack all the harder.

Finally I decided that the time was right to put all I knew to use and to make my move, to take up the offensive. I knew I could not last much longer fighting only on the defensive. I was bleeding from half a dozen minor wounds and I was tiring, but my opponent was also getting weary. I marshaled my remaining energy and struck hard and fast with the utmost determination.

At first this renewed action on my part surprised the warrior and threw him back. The shock on his face was now evident for me to see, but soon he regained his ground and was at me again. He was a persistent fellow, I'll give him that.

By this time both of us were using every trick and gambit we knew to outdo the other, yet neither of us could gain the upper hand for more than a few moments. We fought on for a good half hour, an incredible amount of time in this kind of heated battle, and both of us were now obviously exhausted.

Finally, I knew that my plan was working. By my lasting with him, I had gained the edge and now my opponent even had to acknowledge that fact as he gasped at me in awe. It was then for the first time that my blade drove through his guard and nicked him drawing blood!

It was red blood, so I knew he was certainly human after all.

Then I nicked him again!

Then yet again for a third time!

Now I saw the nervous look on the young warrior's face, and I knew that he realized that I finally had him. I had bested him and his life was mine, should I desire to take it. But I did not want to do that. There had to be a better way to end this and not kill such a brave adversary.

This warrior was a brave men, he did not panic, but fought steadfastly onward, doing the best he could as I pushed him back, nicked him here or there, threatened his heart with my blade many times. He was surprised and concerned. I knew what that meant. He was wondering who I was, who it was who could be besting him? He was a talented swordsman, one of the best I had ever encountered, but now our contest was ending.

Then I cut him good, a deeper wound that shocked him so that he came at me in rage with all that he had left. It wasn't nearly enough. Unfortunate for him, but he did try his best and I give him credit for that. He pushed me back twenty feet, I lunged forward, caught his sword, lifted it up and pulled it out of his hand.

He shouted in anger, then looked at me with shock and awe. Now he was unarmed and at my mercy.

Instantly I was upon him with my bayonet to his throat.

The warrior just stared at me, apparently unable to believe that I had bested him. He muttered some strange words which I did not understand in some foreign language I did not know. I just shook my head and he repeated the words again more urgently. I wish I knew what he was saying, but I did not.

I now noticed that the lovely green-haired girl was terrified by what had happened, even more surprised than the warrior himself at my victory in our fight. None more surprised than I, of course, at that point for I had been a bit rusty on my fencing skills. Then the girl screamed loud and furiously at me.

The warrior looked up into my eyes, my blade still at his throat, as if o say, "Why don't you just end it! Run your blade across my throat!"

I could not do that to an unarmed man, nor to such a brave and talented opponent. I am a soldier, a warrior in my own way, much as he is. I am not a killer. I am certainly no executioner. And if the truth be told I kind of liked this young warrior. He was certainly brave, and he had fought me fairly, which is something one warrior appreciates in another—that sense of honor—in an enemy or opponent that matters greatly to all those who have ever been in battle. Furthermore, the idea of killing an unarmed and helpless man, even if he might be my enemy, was abhorrent to me and went against everything I believed in as a fighting man. The truth was that it was I who was the enemy here. After all, I was the invader in his world, not he in mine.

So I decided to take a chance on the look of character I could plainly see in the young man's face. He appeared to be a man of honor and he had shown honor in his fight with me. I lowered my point from his throat and slowly put my bayonet back into my boot. Then I picked up his sword and handed it back to him.

I saw his face brighten but it was more confused than ever at my strange action. For I was to learn later that mercy was a luxury that while not all that common on Earth, was obviously rarer still on this strange world.

I was about to congratulate myself on my decision when suddenly my head exploded into a volcano of pain and all went black as I sank into unconsciousness.

CHAPTER 3

ZAOR AND SIRAH

How long I was unconscious I did not know. When I awoke I found myself in utter darkness, and with a splitting headache.

I called out and soon a large wooden door was opened, and with it came a bright string of outside daylight stabbing down at me. I shielded my eyes until they became accustomed to the light.

A man entered the chamber. I saw now that it was the same green-skinned warrior who I had crossed swords with outside in the clearing. As he came closer he drew his sword and spoke to me calmly but firmly.

Well, here I thought, might be the end of me. Tied and bound, like a helpless babe, it appeared to me that I was going to receive the terrible end that I had spared this warrior. It was not fair, but nothing in life and war is fair. It appeared I was to be executed while unarmed and helpless!

I looked up at his eyes boldly, my face a torrid mixture of rage and hopelessness—and filled with impending doom. And a dark sadness that it had all come to this after so long.

The warrior advanced on me, coming closer and closer and I closed my eyes and awaited the killing blow. I had seen the sunlight reflecting off the keen edge of his sharp blade, and I knew that soon I would taste that cold hard steel and that it would drink deeply of my blood. So be it! I was resigned to my fate now, alone on an alien world, what did it matter?

Then to my utter astonishment the warrior came right up to me, gave me a slight grin, then stooped down and cut my bonds. I was released! It was a most welcome and surprising action, and the sudden thought struck me then that I might not be executed, and that I might just live long enough to see that stunning green-haired girl once again.

Then the warrior quickly motioned me to get up and follow him.

Soon, escorted by two more burly warriors who followed closely behind me, I was taken like a young lamb to who knew what strange fate.

Now that I could see the outside world again—even if it wasn't my own world—I began to feel a renewed sense of optimism. I was alive! I still lived! I looked around me and wondered at that strange red sky and bright red sun overhead. I knew this was not some terrible dream, but some much more terrible and possibly deadly, reality. I could see towering black and brown mountains, green and red trees, and an abundance of bright colors everywhere. The fresh air was cool and crisp and clean, and I luxuriated in the deep breathes I took of the cool free air. I enjoyed it while I had the chance.

Then I froze as I saw the beautiful green-haired girl when I was escorted past a place where she was working. I noticed that she was skinning some strange unearthly hide with several other girls and women. She was a real looker all right. Tall and slim, with a gorgeous body and the face of an angel. All the time she must have been watching me as well, for as I turned to see her, she quickly looked away and suddenly buried herself with the work before her. Obviously she had been watching me, just as I had been watching her. I wondered what she was like and what her name might be.

However, I had little time for those musings now. I was driven through the village by the young warrior and my guards. This village that I was being led through was actually a motley conglomeration of caves cut into the black and brown mountains. These caves appeared to run into the rock quite deep and intricate, with passages and tunnels honeycombing these mountains. I saw many hundreds of children and women around the large open area at the mouth of these caves and caverns, which all seemed to circle what I took for the center of this village, a huge common area.

One interesting aspect of this village was that nowhere did I ever see any old people, which at the time I thought most strange. No old men, no old women at all. It didn't make any sense to me at the time. I also noticed an absence of younger and middle-aged men. I wondered, if perhaps, they were out hunting or engaged in some warrior mission? But the absence of the old had me intrigued. It seemed there was no one over fifty years of age there at all.

However, at this point in my adventure I had more important things on my mind than mere theories of otherworldly anthropology, as interesting as I thought a study of this society of cave-dwelling mountain folk might be. I was now being held as some kind of prisoner, not in any immediate danger it appeared, but my prospects seemed very dicey.

It wasn't long before the warrior brought me into a well lit cave. It was larger than most of the others and inside it was empty. No people and not very many furnishings. I was brought inside and securely tied to large metal rings in the wall. Then the three warriors walked out of the cave and I was left alone.

Well this was a pretty pickle! Once again, I was alone and helpless and I did not like it. However my solitude did not last long, for an hour later the green-haired girl I had seen twice before entered the cave. I was shocked to see her and awed by her beauty. She was so beautiful, with lovely long, straight-shiny green hair that glistened with raven highlights in the brilliant sunlight. Her lips were green—perhaps some form of lip gloss, which I was eager to find out—as were her eyebrows. The effect was entrancing. She came over to me and looked at me carefully, cautiously but with some interest, as if examining some kind of wild but dangerous animal. She was careful not to get too close to me, for I could see she was scared of me, but I could tell she was intrigued by me also. In any event she had nothing at all to fear from me. And there was something else there, I saw it in her eyes, and I hoped that it was what I thought it was. For I believe we both felt it, it was nothing less that a powerful physical attraction that seemed to bond us together as neither of us had ever felt before in our lives. Well, I certainly felt it, and I hoped she did also.

I gave the girl a polite hello, but of course she could not understand my words. So I took a chance and flashed her a friendly smile, and she haltingly smiled back, so I felt I had at least broken the ice. Eventually I gave up speaking to her, it was just too frustrating and difficult. I would have to wait until a time when she would be able to understand my words, or I hers. I knew now that my first priority if I survived my capture here, the most important aspect of my survival on this strange world, must be to learn the language of these people. I only wondered if my captors would teach me their language. In fact, at this point, I wondered if I would be kept alive long enough to even learn my first word of their language.

When she went away from me I felt more alone than I have ever felt in my life.

I couldn't help but allow my thoughts to stray to the face and form of that lovely green-haired girl though. She was a healthy and happy young woman, a real beauty in the prime of life. I watched her with a fine smile as I saw her busy herself with the cutting and mixing of certain dried meats and vegetables. These soon went into a large cooking pot which she had one of the men bring into the cave. When the pot was full, she put it on the fire built of logs and ringed with stones, then she went out of the cave for a short time. I'm sure she realized that all the while she was working, my eyes never left her gorgeous face and form.

When the woman came back into the cavern, it was with the warrior I had fought in the clearing the day before. I assumed that this must be his cave. The girl, I had to admit with obvious disappointment, was probably the man's wife. They seemed near the same age and quite friendly. I saw that she seemed to be the women who cooked for him and did all his household work. So it seemed a natural assumption she might be his woman.

Or was she?

After diner, for which I was thankfully given a good-size share of tasty meat and vegetable mush, and even though it annoyed me to be tied up and spoon-fed like a baby by the girl—it did have its advantages. The closer she got to me the more I was entranced by her presence, and I could see that she seemed to be interested in me the same way as well. This was certainly good for starters. We smiled at each other, we laughed—she had a delightful laugh—and we tried to communicate but to no avail.

As the girl fed me, the warrior came over and looked me over carefully up and down. He was inspecting me, examining me. Obviously trying to figure out who and what I was, and where the hell I had come from. He clearly had never seen anyone quite like me before and I had plainly never seen anyone like him or these people before.

Once again the warrior spoke his strange words to me, but I could not understand what he was saying and made it plain to him. I was relieved to see that he did not become angry this time, merely puzzlement and curiosity writ large upon his features. Then the warrior, with the help of the girl, continued at this for some time, asking me questions, mouthing strange words at me again and again. Then speaking more words to me and repeating them, with the idea that I should repeat the words they spoke to me. I did so. They pointed to various objects and spoke a word, then had me repeat it. Then they said more strange words, looking at me, pointing, repeating the words, then questions and phrases. In this way I began my education on this strange new world to learn the language of these fascinating people. I proved an eager student and wanted to learn all I could. I knew such knowledge and my ability to communicate with these people would make the difference between life and death for me. But I had other motives—notably that lovely green-haired woman who I could not get out of my thoughts.

While all this was going on, a large heavily-bearded giant of a warrior entered the cave and came over to where we were seated. This man looked to be the oldest male of the group I had yet seen here, he looked to be at least forty years of age, and he had numerous scars upon his massive body. Some might say these scars attested to his prowess in battle, but being a warrior I knew that all it really meant was that he had taken a lot of beatings. However, I was not cocky enough to dismiss the fact that he had obviously given a lot of scars—and worse—to his opponents in battle as well. He was a dangerous looking fellow, and did not seem to be in any good humor. His hand was on the hilt of his sword as he came closer to look at me. I was still bound, and he was careful nonetheless as he came close to examine me.

The giant nodded, talked to the warrior and then to the girl, who seemed to fear him. In fact, it was apparent that neither the warrior nor the girl seemed to like this giant very much, but he was evidently some important leader in this tribe or village. The giant certainly had a mean and nasty look to him, and I saw the look full force when he came over to me and stared at me menacingly. I know I must have appeared pretty strange to him with my military khaki jungle fatigues and heavy U.S. Army boots. My bayonet had been taken away from me earlier, along with my .45. Nevertheless, I must have looked pretty wild-eyed and disheveled to them then.

Maybe dangerous too. My white skin contrasted with their own green hued skin and was obviously a subject of rabid conjecture among them.

Carefully the giant examined me, poking and prodding me as his eyes bore down upon me with menacing looks of abject hatred. I had no idea why he was so belligerent towards me, but he surely seemed to be. He growled and shouted to me in a language that of course I could not understand. Upon no reply from me, he growled again, repeated the question even louder as if I were deaf, and he was just about to slap my face when the girl said something that stopped him. She probably reminded him that I could not speak or understand their language. The giant boiled with range now, I can only imagine that it was because of my ignorance of his esteemed personage, for which he gave me a swift hard punch to the ribs. The pain flowed over my body.

I took it. Stone silent. But I would remember it.

I saw the sadness on the face of the young warrior and the girl that I should be abused so. They did not approve of that at all, and that gave me some hope. That spoke well for them. But I was ready to fight back and knock this giant's block off, if I was ever released and got the chance to do so.

I shouted, "Big man when you hit me while I'm chained and helpless! Why not release me, then see what I do to you!"

Had I not been tied and helpless my attacker would have had something very serious to worry about. Attacking a helpless enemy will not win you points in my book. And when I am that victim, I will fight back and fight back hard.

I noticed that the young warrior now seemed to protest his leader's action and soon some kind of heated argument ensued between the two, during which the girl came over beside me to inspect the injury to my ribs and to see if they were broken. They were not broken, but they were bruised and sure hurt like hell. I would remember what this giant had done to me and payback would be sweet.

The only good part of this entire incident was to have the girl with me by my side. So close. So caring about my treatment and my injury. For I could see now that she was just as repelled by the giant's cowardly attack upon me as was her companion, the young warrior.

I smiled at her again, but then she withdrew so the giant could not see, turning her face away from me. However, when I smiled at her once more, she smiled back and it was truly lovely to behold. It was such a beautiful smile that, had I been able, I could have kissed her right then and there.

The young warrior, and the giant who was the leader, continued to argue. Then all of a sudden, the giant barked a command and left the cave. Now the warrior came over to the girl and spoke to her swiftly, giving her some kind of order. It was from that night onward that I began to be taught their language.

CHAPTER 4

SIRAH

The girl proved to be patient and a good teacher. I could not ask for anyone better to teach me her language and customs, and it was a most pleasant association for me, and I think for her, too.

We began with names. The girl pointed to herself and told me her name was "Sirah." I smiled and repeated her name. It sounded wonderful upon my lips. She smiled, while the warrior who was also with her now, nodded. He hit his chest and said "Zaor." I nodded, said his name, then pointed to myself and said "Jon Kirk."

It was not long before we were pointing at a multitude of objects. Sirah would tell me their names, and I would repeat the strange sounds that made up what was her language. We did this day in and day out, working hour after hour.

It took at least a month of constant drilling and study for me to learn Sirah's language well enough so that I could make myself understood when I spoke to her and to Zaor. But I learned the basics after the first few days. During all that time I remained tied to that cave wall, away from the warmth of the bloody red sun overhead. I couldn't wait for the day I would be allowed to be released from these chains and let out of this cave to be a free man again. I worked hard at my language lessons so that I would see that day as soon as possible.

Over those long weeks Sirah and I talked of many things, and eventually Zaor, Sirah, and I became fast friends. We all seemed to like and respect each other from the start, but my interest in Sirah was much more than mere friendship, though I felt it wise to be prudent and silent on that score for now.

Occasionally the other girl I had seen when first I had come here, the red-haired girl, whose name I learned was Manalia, also came to visit in the cave. I was happy, actually relieved to discover that she seemed to be a lover of Zaor's, yet was also very friendly with his mate, Sirah. Did Zaor have two wives? My happiness of a moment before was crushed by this thought. For the time being I put all these confusing questions out of my head. I did not want to complicate matters and concentrated on learning this new language and the customs of these people. I worked hard and long and Sirah proved a good teacher. It wasn't long before we were all talking together like old friends, exchanging information about our worlds and lives. It was at that time I decided to ask Zaor if he would release me. He told me that Tob, the giant who I had met that night weeks ago, was their king and had left very specific orders about me.

Zaor said sadly, "Tob gave me orders to keep you chained here and teach you our language. One day, he told me, he will come back here with his army and if you are not here he will burn our village and put everyone to the sword. He is a serious man, a man of no honor, but he is not to be trifled with."

On that cheery note I put off my plans of escape. For any escape by me would surely doom these good people and I did not want to do that. Instead, I concentrated on learning their language and anything I could about this new world of theirs—and now mine.

Time passed and I found out much about this new world and my new friends Zaor, Manalia, and Sirah.

Sirah, the beautiful, green-haired green girl.

Here are some of the things I learned that I put away in my mind for use if need be, if I ever escaped and became free. I learned that the name for this world was Ares, and that we were in the Coastal Mountains, and that I had fallen into hands of a tribe of the outlawed Caste of Warriors. It seemed that all warriors on the planet lived hidden in these mountains, in which the giant, King Tob ruled. When I asked who it was that these warriors were hiding from I was met with a dark and grim shudder from Sirah and Zaor.

Zaor then told me about the Zarans, the weird flying Winged-men of Ares.

"They are monsters!" Zaor said seriously, his face clouding over with intense hatred. "They are flying beasts and are the great fear and oppressors of all the people of Ares. For thousands of years, millions of people on our world have been killed or captured by them, enslaved and sent to Zaran cities. To this day none of those taken have ever returned. No one knows what happens to these luckless individuals. It is a jealously guarded secret that the Zaran masters do not allow to be known. But there are, like all things concerning the mysterious Zarans, rumors. Terrible rumors to scare small children, and that put fear in all adults as well."

I digested this information as Zaor told me about the other tribes of Ares, such as the many trade groups that inhabit different areas of the planet. They each seek to live as far away from the dread Zaran Winged-men as possible. Yet it does them no good. All people of Ares tremble when they hear the fateful clap of leathery flying wings overhead.

To the coast, below the mountains, Zaor told me there lived the Castes of Woodworkers, and the Stonecutters, while in the lush lands of the south were the various Castes of Farmers, each group a specialist in growing a particular food. In the north were various Castes of Animal Herders, while above the mountains were Castes of Miners, Clothworkers, and the Metal Workers who made such fine weapons for the Warrior Castes. All of these included traders who sold goods for their particular caste or clan or village.

It seemed the Zaran Winged-men rarely flew into the mountains. It was too easy for them to be ambushed in the low valleys and ravines, and also because most of these people had nothing the Zarans really wanted that badly. So as long as members of the Warrior Caste did not fight back against them and stayed in exile in the mountains the Zarans did not bother them overly much. Nevertheless, that did not mean the Winged-men never came into the mountains. The Winged-men went where they would on the planet Ares and they did what they wanted to do. On those few times they did fly into the mountain areas, they killed everyone they could or captured all those that were left alive from their raid. Those that did not escape or were captured as slaves were always killed.

While I had never seen any of these Zaran Winged-men since my advent upon Ares, Zaor and Sirah made drawings for me. Sirah and others gave me detailed descriptions of them. They certainly seemed fearsome. They really did fly, and they were not human at all!

From Zaor's description and definition of their actions the Zarans seemed a terrible and frightful group of vicious winged monsters. As yet I had not seen one, and I hoped that I never would for the stories I heard about them fairly froze the blood in the veins of the most ferocious warriors.

Zaor told me that once, in the distant past, Ares had a great civilization of the green-skinned human races, until the Zarans had come. How they had arrived on Ares no one knew, but legend said they fell to the surface in long shiny tubes with one end that was on fire.

To me that seemed as good as description of a rocket ship as any I have ever heard. So they had come to Ares from another world!

The Zaran ships must have come as invaders or perhaps had crashed somehow, and the original survivors settled on Ares, or colonized it. Maybe there were originally some Zaran outposts or cities built at one time, long ago colonies for ships that flew back and forth between Zar and Ares? Who can say for sure that far back. No one seemed to know exactly where Zar was, but I assumed it was another planet in this solar system. At least that was my best guess. Today, there were only six cities left on Ares, on what is known as Cos, the eastern continent, and all were held by the Zaran Winged-men. There was rumor that there was a vast western continent as well. Some called it The Unknown Land, others said it was the land of the blue-hued Vognars, but most of this was rumor among the green peoples. Nowhere else on the continent of Cos did the Zarans allow the green-skinned peoples to have their own city. The green people had been scattered all over the planet, their cities smashed or occupied, and their castes broken or scattered to the far winds and the dark corners of the land.

Once, it was rumored that a long time ago there had been mighty cities of the green peoples, but the Zarans conquered them all and scattered the people of Ares to the four winds. The Zaran Winged-men have preyed upon the green peoples ever since, and the warfare has been so constant that the Aresans never had the chance to build another city that could stand up to the enemy and keep them and their families safe. It was also rumored that the Caste of Warriors, many hundreds of years ago, had gathered together a great army under General Hoam to fight the Zarans and then to build their own city, but soon rival leaders grew greedy and war broke out among the green peoples. War broke out and the green warriors and their hunter allies were, by treachery defeated, then led into the merciless hands of the bloody Zarans and slaughtered.

Afterwards, the few remaining warriors, now a disorganized mass of stragglers and defeated fighters, found themselves pursued until they found refuge in the caves of the Coastal Mountains. With these warriors came their wives and children, sisters and brothers, until each tribe settled throughout the many mountain caves.

Zaor was the chief of his tribal warrior group, known as the Sword Clan, which consisted of some five thousand people. Many other tribes or clans like his existed, scattered and hidden all throughout the mountain vastness. They lived in constant fear of the Zarans and the dread flap-flap-flap of leather wings bringing death from above. It was a terrible sound of swooping doom. It could cause a green-skinned child to cry, or freeze the blood in the veins of the most seasoned warrior.

Of all these various warrior tribes and chieftains, Tob was the hereditary king of them all. He took his kingship in a direct line from the last human commander of Ares, General Hoam. Zaor also told me that King Tob was nothing like his esteemed ancestor who was known as Hoam The Hero. Tob was cowardly and treacherous, a liar and worse, a bully and a leader who only cared for his own needs and not those of his people. It was only Tob's great talent for treachery and fighting prowess and size, that had kept him the king for so long.

"Just how long has Tob been your king?" I asked.

"His reign has been short, no more than four kloms," Zaor told me. I figured it out one night, and if I had been correct, I was astounded. For it meant that Tob had been king of the Warrior Caste for four hundred Earth years!

"Four hundred years?" I whispered to myself, amazed. I realized that would make Tob almost 450 Earth years old. How could that be? It was just another of those amazing and strange realities that I had encountered since I had come to the weird world of Ares. It all seemed so incredible and I asked Zaor about it the next morning.

"As far as anyone can tell, by your time system where one of our klom is 100 of your years—Tob is almost 690 years old," Zaor corrected me. Then he looked at me and smiled. "Why are you so shocked, Jon Kirk? Do not people on your home of Earth live this length of time?"

"No, not at all" I replied sharply, shaking my head in wonder. "My friend, our life span is much shorter on Earth. For instance, I have lived only 25 years."

Zaor laughed at that admission," Why you are but a pup, Jon Kirk! Why, my sister, Sirah, is even older than you are! She is still a youth, but almost ninety years old by your time frame."

"Zaor!" a loud feminine voice called out in mock anger. It was Sirah. "How dare you tell this man my age!"

Zaor and I just laughed in good fellowship at her words. It appeared to me that women are much the same on whatever world you find them. Even Sirah joined in on our laughter.

From that day on I was able to get things figured out a bit better and was happy to note that Sirah was Zaor's younger sister, and not his mate. His mate, though they had not formally mated in the Ares sense, was Manalia. This made me very happy to hear that Sirah was not Zaor's wife, and it caused me much relief. For I now realized that Sirah was a free woman. And the fact that she was almost ninety years old didn't mean a thing to me at all. Why, she didn't look a day over twenty-one!

And then there was King Tob. Now what of him? He was the ruler and King of the Warrior Caste and had been so for over four hundred years! It was astonishing to me, yet it was apparently true. There was no mistake.

What I was also later told, explained the lack of old people among the green races that I had noticed since I had come among these people. Most Ares green people can easily live a life span that can run a thousand Earth years or more. However, once they reach that late stage of life, the aging process advances exponentially. In fact, it advances so rapidly that at that stage of life an old person will soon become ill and continue to age at a fantastic rate of speed. Within weeks or months that person will be dead.

It seemed strange to me that age did not matter here on Ares except for the very old. An Ares green-skinned person at age one-hundred, five-hundred, or even nine-hundred, will look as young and be as vigorous as an Earthling of but twenty years of age. Any one of them at any age could pass for a young man or woman of Earth, but for the greenish hue of their skin and the red or green color of their hair. However, an Ares man of a thousand-eighty years or eleven-hundred years in age would soon appear as old as an Earthling of ninety or a hundred years of age and not have more than a few months of life left after that. All in all, the Ares aging process did not stop after the thousandth year of life, it only proceeded at an incredibly accelerated rate.

Of course, all during this time I was learning the language and history of Ares, I was still being held a prisoner in that cave. I had talked with Zaor about many things. I asked him about releasing my bonds upon my word of honor that I would not leave the cave, nor try to escape. I gave him my word freely and intended to keep it, not wanting to do anything to put these fine people in jeopardy with their ruthless king. Zaor told me he trusted my word and he released my bonds. It was a great relief. It certainly was an improvement in my captivity to be able to move around, and if I could not go out and sit in the sun, I could at least stand in the entrance of the cave and look outside at the red orb overhead, feel its warmth, feel the free wind upon my face, and breathe the cool, crisp mountain air. I could still look out at the far horizon and dream...of freedom.

Some day.

It was the third day after I had been released from my chains and allowed the freedom of the cave, and I was standing at the entrance, watching Sirah at work below preparing the daily meal like she did every day. Zaor had gone out hunting with all the men of his village. Later on Sirah was in the clearing below with the other women of the tribe sewing hides together for clothing and cutting vegetables. Since I had become a prisoner, I had removed my hot and uncomfortable Earth army fatigues and boots for the lighter single hides and laced sandals of these mountain people.

By then my gun and bayonet had been returned to me by Zaor. He told me that the items were my property and should rightfully be returned to me and for that I was most thankful. How thankful, I would soon have occasion to show. In fact, it would prove a momentous piece of luck for all of us that I was given back my Earthly weapons.

The bayonet, Zaor was well familiar with, as to him it was but a short sword or dagger, he also knew it quite well through our fight. He knew first-hand it could prove a most dangerous weapon.

However, regarding my .45 auto, I believe he thought that was merely some kind of fancy war club. I knew only too well that my .45 could prove my ace in the hole here on Ares, and I decided I would not tell anyone of its true power.

I believe Zaor trusted me not to escape as I had promised him, and I decided to honor my promise, as I always do. To be sure, even if I did escape, where would I go? There was no way I could ever get back home to Earth. I still knew very little about Ares, so where would I go? What would I do? Even if I wasn't killed by savages or Tob's men, then I would surely be killed by the even more savage beasts that roamed these mountains at night. Or perhaps one of the Zaran Winged-men would end my life? Regardless of the many problems I saw in escaping, quite simply, I did not want to escape just yet. I had given and promise, but even more so, I had made some good friends here, and I was treated well.

And then there was Sirah.

By this time Sirah and I seemed to be getting along quite well, or at least, I thought we were, though she kept warning me about Tob and his ill temper. She was always friendly to me and I could tell she was holding back on her emotions. I wondered why. Then one day she surprised me by saying outright that Tob wanted her for his mate, and that I should be careful of him. Upon hearing that I told her that Tob should be careful of *me!*

"Please be serious! Tob is very jealous, Jon Kirk," Sirah warned me in a soft, sad voice, "and he would just as surely kill you as look at you. I would not like that. It was only through my brother Zaor's insistence on keeping you alive that you were saved at all. Zaor is Tob's bravest chief and hence one of his most valued and influential clan leaders whose wishes can not easily be ignored. But he is not all-powerful, he can not protect you forever and once Tob returns…"

I asked Sirah if my death would bother her and she just looked sad and said, "Jon Kirk, what cannot be, simply cannot be. Were I a free woman… But I am not. The king wants me. So to answer your question, yes your death would pain me deeply, but I am promised to Tob."

That knowledge devastated me and I felt terrible. A great darkness overcame me at just the thought of my lovely Sirah with that loathsome fiend.

The next day Sirah began working on a new set of skins for me. When she was finished she came up to the cave entrance where I usually stood looking out over the valley, waiting for her as I watched her work. She came up to the cave and stood very close to me and handed me the new skins. They were soft and finely made.

"Thank you," I said with a smile, as she presented then to me, and then it happened. We looked into each others eyes and it seemed for that moment as if we were the only people in the world. Slowly I put my arms around her lean waist and pulled her to me until her luscious green full lips were locked onto mine. Then we were holding each other tightly and kissing at the cave entrance as if we'd been doing it all our lives. It was our first kiss and it was a moment of bliss I shall never forget.

Suddenly from below us there was a loud commotion and louder shouts. Sirah and I were too busy to really care or notice, until a booming voice from behind me gave out with an enraged yell.

"Sirah! Sirah get away from that pig!"

It was King Tob, and behind him were a hundred of his most fierce warriors.

Sirah opened her eyes, and I shot a glance behind me just in time to see a large blade coming down at my head. Instantly I pulled Sirah away to safety as I dodged the blow by rolling away on the ground.

I quickly drew my bayonet, and hearing the footsteps of my attacker behind me, I jumped to my feet ready to meet Tob, blade to blade.

CHAPTER 5

KING OF THE WARRIOR CASTE

King Tob was wielding a massive, two-handed broadsword, his giant arms slashing it at me again and again. He was like an out-of-control wild bull. I knew that Tob was a formidable warrior, regardless of what was said about his honor and bravery. He was large and powerful and knew how to use his weapons. I was lucky, or skillful enough in this initial attack and was able to dodge his charges and ward off his blows. I would have instantly had to forfeit my life had any of those powerful blows connected.

All I had to defend myself with was my trusty bayonet, a good weapon, but nothing compared to Tob's massive sword. I didn't want to use my .45 yet, but I was ready to withdraw it and use it should things get too hairy. It was good to know that I had that weapon to fall back on if I needed it.

Tob was a giant, powerful and mean, and armed with a killer weapon that could easily cut me in half if he ever got close enough to use it. Nevertheless, his huge size and the massive weapon he wielded did tend to slow him down, while my own slim blade—just two feet in length—was easily maneuverable. I knew that I might have a chance against Tob, if he didn't catch me with that monstrous blade of his!

The fight between us raged on. It was fast and furious. A few moments more and I would have been done for, but then, through the large crowd of onlookers came another group of warriors. In a quick sidewise glance I noticed Zaor at their lead. I felt a wave of relief but it was short lived. Tob took full advantage of the distraction and knocked me down with a particularly vicious blow. To my horror my weapon was flung out of my hand. Now I was down and unarmed!

Tob saw that I was helpless and vulnerable and let out a vicious laugh that promised my doom. He came at me then, close, closer. I remembered my .45 and reached for it, withdrawing it and raising it for use. Tob, no doubt, thought it was some kind of fancy war club. He let out another contemptuous laugh at what he thought my feeble attempt to defend myself.

"Tob! If you want to fight someone, fight me!" Zaor shouted, drawing his own blade now in challenge as he strode towards the giant warrior king.

Tob turned away from me and stared at Zaor in anger and surprise.

"This is rebellion! Treason!" Tob warned in rage, but then he looked over at me, then back at Zaor curiously. The man was up to something. Suddenly Tob spoke up, "But, friend, Zaor, put down your weapon, this stranger should not make us fight amongst ourselves. Let us talk this over peacefully."

"That would be a good idea," Zaor said, and my gut wrenched when I saw him lower his sword, even as Tob lowered his own weapon.

Both men made the Ares sign of peace, clenched fist over the heart, and approached each other warily...

"Careful, Zaor!" Sirah and Manalia whispered fearfully. "We all know full well of Tob's treachery."

Tob pointed to me, but he spoke to Zaor.

"Yonder pig of a cur stranger attacked your sister," Tob lied bold faced to Zaor. "You know that I want Sirah for myself. Untouched for the mating."

Zaor grew red.

Sirah shouted, "Lair! Dirty liar! It was Tob who attacked Jon Kirk! Zaor, it was Jon Kirk who defended me from the ravishing of Tob!"

Zaor looked at his sister and seemed to boil over in rage now. I wasn't sure what was going to happen or what he would do. However, before he could act, in a lightning quick maneuver, Tob grabbed Sirah and placed a dagger at her perfect throat. He then ordered Zaor and his men to move back away from him. Tob called his own warriors to come forward, his personal guard, and they stood at his side forming an impenetrable wall around their leader.

"Help me, Jon Kirk!" Sirah cried out in terror, and I almost went insane with anger and frustration when I saw Tob cuff her across the face for her words. He had knocked her into unconsciousness and I boiled over with rage. At that moment I think I went crazy with blind hatred for Tob and vowed that I would someday kill him.

But not just yet. For neither I nor anyone else could get near Tob or his men, and he still held a dagger at Sirah's throat.

This was a brutal form of treachery that I had never known before and Zaor and I could only watch helplessly as we followed behind Tob and his men as they stole away in an attempt to escape.

Zaor was in a bad way worrying over the safety of his sister, and I was insane with rage not knowing if I would ever see the lovely Sirah again. Knowing only too well the horrible fate that Tob had in store for my beloved should he ever make her his mate.

We could not rush or attack Tob and his men, nor could we provoke the king for fear of his hurting Sirah. Zaor assured me that the king and his warriors were entirely capable of dispatching Sirah without a thought, right before our eyes should we make the mistake of pressing them too hard. So it was a standoff and Tob and his warriors were allowed to quickly retreat from us and we could do nothing but watch them go as they melted into the night.

At this time when I though all was lost, I noticed that Saok's hunting party had just returned to the village, and I could see that Saok sensed what had occurred. Saok was fiercely independent but very loyal, he was a valiant warrior and also a good friend to Zaor and Sirah. He was a sub-chief of the Sword Clan.

Upon Saok's orders his men quickly threw down their kills, drew their swords, and then charged at Tob's men. In complete surprise they fell upon the rear guard of Tob's fleeing group.

It was instant chaos now, and had become open civil war among the various clans of the Warrior Caste. Such an event could only benefit the Zarans, and make the Warrior Caste weaker with much shedding of blood and ill feelings, but there was nothing else to do about it now but fight.

Fight to win!

Fight against Tob!

Fight to save Sirah!

Tob and his clan had to be defeated, so now it was civil war amongst the clans of the Warrior Caste.

With the added men from Saok's clan the two sides in the conflict were now almost even in the amount of warriors. Now the clearing below the caves became a mass of bloody battle and death. Women ran, children screamed, warriors yelled blood-curdling war cries as they charged other men from other warrior clans with bloody weapons.

Zaor and I found ourselves fighting two shaggy warriors from Tob's band. We were trying our best to dispatch these men so we could then get closer to Tob. He was wisely surrounded by his best warriors, protected in the center of his swordsmen as he urged them on to victory against us. Tob had long since thrown down the unconscious Sirah to the ground in an effort to defend himself when one of Saok's men broke through the ranks and made a bold attack on him. That brave warrior had been quickly killed. It had been a mad suicide attack, but Tob had also been wounded and it was obvious to us he was in shock now that one of his own former warriors had been able to come so close to killing him.

I saw that Zaor was fighting intensely with another man now, so now it would only be I who would have to come to Sirah's aid. I was able to reach her quickly, dispatching another of Tob's men, then I picked up her prone form, and carried her away to the entrance to a nearby cave. At that point I set her carefully down on a blanket and Manalia, Zaor's mate, came forward with other women of the clan to take care of her.

"Guard her well!" I told Manalia, now relieved that Sirah was in safe hands and being taken care of. She seemed well and was regaining consciousness. Now I could get back to the battle. For I had a score to settle with King Tob.

When I reached the king of the Warrior Caste I saw that he had just finished gutting one of our men, a lad who I had noticed was young and inexperienced but who fought heroically. As Tob withdrew his blood-soaked sword from the corpse of the dead warrior I called out to him.

"Turn and face me!" I shouted moving towards him. "It is your time to die!"

Tob turned, saw me, and froze. I could feel the fear of the man, the cowardice ooze out of him. He recognized me as the same warrior he had fought previously, the same man who had been his prisoner, so now that somehow allowed him to regain his courage. He then laughed his guttural piggish laugh.

Then Tob came at me with raised sword and a loud lusty roar. I was ready for him. I had put away my bayonet by then and now held my own sword and charged him.

We clashed together in a wild melee. Tob's first swing at me was a terrific blow, his great two-handed broadsword aimed squarely at my head. He had figured to take me out quickly with one massive strike, but he had figured wrong!

I quickly ducked his initial powerful stroke, then turned as my sword found him and sliced him in the side. He ignored the wound, and with a maddened cry of rage Tob came at me once again. It seemed at this point that nothing could stop the rampaging giant. However, this time he had learned to be more cautious, and he held me in a heated battle which neither of us seemed to be winning.

All around us the overall battle raged on between Zaor and his allies and the warriors loyal to Tob, but I noticed that many of Tob's men had been killed, others seemed ready to surrender. It was evident to me that Zaor and his warriors were slowly but surely winning the battle. Then I shuddered with an uncanny feeling of dread, for I suddenly heard a strange sound growing louder and louder, coming closer and closer. It was the loud swooshing of great flapping leather wings!

CHAPTER 6

ATTACK OF THE WINGED-MEN

The flapping grew louder and louder and suddenly from all around me I heard terrible cries and screams of people who were now full of fear and terror.

"The Zarans!" someone yelled frantic. "Run! Run for your life!"

"The Winged-men are here!" another voice shouted in terror. "Run!"

Tob looked up at the approaching enemy as did all of us, and I saw an icy fear overcome his face. I thought he should order a counterattack—call the clans to stop their fighting and join together to fight off the Winged-men invaders—but instead Tob took me completely by surprise once again. His treachery seemed to know no bounds, even for his own tribe and clan. He looked up, eyes full of fear and dread—then he simply ran away. The coward ran away to hide!

I stood there alone and stunned by his action, but my surprise was short-lived, for no sooner did I catch my breathe and realize what had happened than the Winged-men came at us with swords reigning death from above. They struck down at us from overhead. It was almost impossible to fight them off. Some of the more bolder creatures alighted upon the ground and came at our warriors on foot with their swords. The Winged-men on the ground viciously attacked our troops as their brothers overhead cut down our warriors.

All around me Winged-men were landing and engaging in battle with my fellow warriors. Many more of the winged monsters however still flew overhead, raining death down upon our men—men who were helpless to fight back against them. I was relieved to see now that all green men of the Warrior Caste, whether of Tob's faction or Zaor's had joined to fight together against these new invaders, who were for now, our common enemy.

Then I spotted Tob in the distance, he was running into a cave, but I could not get to him as more Winged-men were landing all around us and blocking my pursuit. I grieved for Sirah, for I could not reach her now. Instead I took to fighting the Winged-men as best I could. These winged creatures were definitely humanoid, and seemed almost human in some respects, except for their purple skin tone—and of course the leathery wings attached to their backs. However, upon closer examination, I noticed that they were far from human, their feet were clawed more like those of giant birds, and they had sharp pointed teeth like a shark, and of course upon their backs just over their shoulders, were two large leathery and heavily muscled appendages they used for flight, which I could not help but notice. These, when opened wide, served as wings and enable the creatures to fly like some kind of giant bats. These wings gave the purple-skinned Winged-men a truly frightful appearance and made them formidable and dangerous in battle.

The Winged-men were amongst us now like bloody demons, slashing and cutting in wholesale slaughter. Most of the creatures fighting us were flying in the air over our heads and devastating in their slaughter, for their winged flight gave them a natural advantage to easily smite down many of our brave warriors. In short order the battle turned into a horrible, one-sided melee. I shuddered when I saw Zaor go down with a blow to the back of his skull.

I tried to fight my way over to help my friend, but I was immediately engaged with two gruesome attackers who turned out to be excellent swordsmen. I soon found myself in a battle to the death.

As I fought these two adversaries I was able to catch fleeting glimpses of what was going on around me in the larger battle. There appeared to be some three hundred Winged-men—the hated Zarans as they called themselves—now engaged in heated battle with my green warrior allies. Their large numbers were enabling them to take a heavy toll of our warriors, but our valiant fighters resisted and fought back with unflinching resolve. They were the bravest of the brave and my heart sang with their sword music.

The battle raged on and the green warriors would not give up an inch of ground to the invaders. Eventually many of the winged monsters had enough and began to fly away. It seemed at most, these Winged-men were nothing more than vicious killing animals and great cowards. They were not true warriors at all and not imbued with any warriors spirit I could see. They had no honor. They killed as a horde and once the horde was broken, they fled. Now that they had lost their appetite for the attack—what they thought would be an easy victory—they began to fly away as suddenly as they had come. Yet they took many captives with them. These winged beasts took women mostly, and some of the younger men not yet of adult age. I knew what that meant. Slaves! Or worse! I had heard the dark rumors from Zaor and Sirah, the talk of the use of the green people by the Zarans for breeding stock, and even for food!

The thought filled my soul with icy fear and then I heard a familiar voice scream my name in pleas of dire terror.

"Jon Kirk! Jon Kirk! Save me!"

It was Sirah! My heart pounded as I looked in the direction of that voice and saw her held captive in the clutches of one of the winged monsters. I was too far away to get to her in time, and could only watch hopelessly in frustration as I saw the Winged-men take flight and fly away with her. The creature flew away, I now realized, with the woman I loved.

This all happened in an instant of the time it has taken me to tell you here, so that no sooner did I see the winged monster fly away with Sirah, than I felt a sharp blow where I was suddenly struck from behind and knocked into unconsciousness.

As I went down I remember looking up to take one last loving glance at Sirah and thinking I would never see her again.

"Help me, Jon Kirk! Help me!" I heard her faint voice shout on the distant winds as blackness clogged my mind and all eventually became dark and silent around me.

CHAPTER 7

IMPRISONED AGAIN!

For the second time since I had arrived upon the planet Ares I awoke with a large bump on my head accompanied by a dull throbbing in my brain from a sudden blow to the head. I opened my eyes and found myself in utter darkness, chained to a wall in what appeared to be some moldy and dank prison cell. I wondered just where I might be. The place stunk with the stench of mildew and decay, and lingering death.

I discovered that I was secured in such a way as to allow me some movement within the cell, so that soon I was on my feet. I examined the area, my hands feeling around in the stygian darkness. From what I was able to determine, the cell was some seven feet high and about twenty feet wide. Actually it was fairly spacious by Earth prison standards—but this was no Earth prison.

As I walked towards the door to ascertain the length of the cell, I suddenly tripped over something in the darkness, and fell over what I thought was, of all things, a dead body. However, no sooner had I touched that body than the man let out a terrific howl of rage and came for me with his hands at my throat. I pushed him away quickly and effortlessly, and soon held him helpless with my own hands around his throat.

"Yield!" I demanded. "Yield and I shall not harm you!"

He held fast, growled, tried to get away but my hold on him was firm and he was not going to get away from me.

"Where are we? Who are you?" I demanded.

"By Zar! Is it you? Can it be? What are you doing here? I must have been sleeping" the man's voice spoke to me now out of the pitch darkness of the cell. He laughed, shook his head, "My name is Armen, I am king of the Sar Nomads. And you? You must be the prisoner who was thrown in here the other day."

"Yes, I am he, my name is Jon Kirk," I replied, seeing now that the man was obviously not a threat and so I let him loose. He was just another fellow prisoner. Unable to see his face in the darkness I asked him, "Is there anyone else in this cell besides us?"

"No, Jon Kirk," Armen said softly. "At one time there were a dozen of my best warriors imprisoned in this cell with me. Who knows what old Tar-Gool does with them. Unfortunately, I am sure that we will find that out eventually. For good or ill. For our turn shall come soon enough."

"Our turn?" I asked. "Our turn for what?"

Armen didn't reply but I could tell that the very thought bothered him. It certainly rang ominous for both of us.

I asked, "Who is this Tar-Gool?"

"I do not know. All I know is that he is a crazy old green man," Armen said fearfully. "Some say he is a sorcerer, others that he is some kind of scientist who knows the secrets of the old knowledge. I am not sure who or what he is. Most wise people fear him. Some people fear him even more than they do the dread Zarans!"

"Why is that?" I asked my cell mate, wondering at just what new mess I had gotten myself into here.

"You seem to be a stranger. Where are you from?" Armen asked me, curious now.

"I told you, my name is Jon Kirk," I replied simply. "I am lately of the Caste of Warriors, from Zaor's Sword Clan." I decided against telling the man that I was from Earth, for he would never believe me or only think me mad, and that would mean he would watch me suspiciously or maybe even try to attack me. I did not need to add to my problems here by speaking the incomprehensible truth to someone who might not understand it. In a time like this I needed friends and allies, not men suspicious of my origin who would be my enemies.

"I know the Caste of Warriors," Armen told me in good humor. He looked at me closely, trying to see my face in the darkness. "So tell me, how is my good friend, the noble King Tob?"

I smiled in the darkness, barely able to restrain a grim laugh at what I had just heard. Was this warrior truly telling me he was an actual friend of Tob? I was silent for a moment, I realized the danger of being truthful with him, but then I could not resist speaking my mind no matter what trouble it brought me.

"Tob," I growled in anger, "is a piece of filth who has less honor than the most lowly *chavas*, and he deserves death for his treachery against my beloved Sirah!"

"I see," Armen said in a noncommittal voice.

"I don't care what you see," I blurted, my anger growing. "Furthermore, should I ever get my hands on him he shall be dead a hundred times by my hands. My only hope is that I reach his miserable hide before Zaor does, for I want the pleasure of killing him myself."

Of course I realized that I had spoken foolishly, since Armen had all but told me he was a friend and sword-mate of Tob. Tob seemed to be some kind of ally of Armen or his clan. I just shrugged and waited for his reaction to my words. Whether it be in harsh words, or attack. So be it! Perhaps I regretted my foolish mistake, but not my words.

Armen had been silent for a long moment, then he broke out in wild laughter, unable to hold back his mirth, "Well said, Jon Kirk! If I had any doubt about you before, it is all gone now."

I looked at his face closely and though I could see him smiling, and I sighed in relief. I liked this fellow, Armen, and did not wish to have him as an enemy.

"Jon Kirk, Tob is a filthy coward who has deserved death in a hundred painful forms," Armen told me suddenly, with fierce anger. "Zaor is a friend-brother to me. I have told him for years to rebel against Tob's rule and slay his chieftan. I have told Zaor to take the kingship, but I know that Zaor's loyalty, and his sworn warrior oath, are ideals he will not go back on, even for the good of his own people and clan."

I nodded, then said, "You know Zaor well, and his noble sense of honor. I have a story to tell you, if you have a mind to listen."

Armen nodded, laughing, "Go ahead, Jon Kirk, tell me your story. You have, as they say, a captive audience."

Then I sat down with Armen and told him all that had happened since the fight with Tob's men in their mountain fastness, the beginning of the civil war among the Warrior Caste, and the sudden murderous attack by the Winged-men.

It was with a sad heart that I told Armen I had seen Zaor struck down in the battle, and I presumed him to be dead, and that Sirah—my lovely Sirah—had been carried off a captive of the Winged-men. Both these events had torn me apart. I thought of brave Zaor, my only friend on this foreign world, now dead. I thought of the lovely Sirah in the clutches of the brutal Winged-men. It was almost too much for me to think about and telling it all to Armen made me relive the horror and the sad feelings that were within me.

Once Armen heard my story he grew sad and angry. He knew Sirah, and he was a friend to her, and of course Zaor and he had been warrior-brothers. "I am sorry to hear this, Jon Kirk. You must steel yourself, for you must know that the Winged-men take captives only for one reason."

"As slaves?" I asked fearfully.

Armen was silent for a long moment, then he replied, "You could say that, at least initially it is slavery, but it ends up far worse, my friend. You see, the Winged-men use their captives for food!"

I did not answer his words for I knew Armen was telling me the truth. I could feel the truth of his words. Of course I found this out later from first-hand experience, the Winged-men lived on the flesh of green people. The green humans. They ate human flesh. It was almost exclusive to their diet. They were carnivorous predators, and they were not human, but some other form of humanoid type life that preyed upon the green people of Ares.

I stood in rage and frustration, for now my mind was full of horror for the fate of my beloved Sirah. I vowed then to kill every Winged beast on Ares if I had to, to get my Sirah back.

* * * *

A period of time passed in our prison cell. I do not know how long it was. Four guards in strange uniforms came into our cell and gave us food. It was a thin gruel with hard bread but we devoured it like it was a sumptuous feast. Since then we were given food twice more. We never knew how long we were imprisoned, but Armen had been brought into the cell a few days before I had been, so it must have been many days.

Nevertheless, time passed, and Armen and I talked over many things. With nothing much else to do all day, all we had to do was talk, and plan, and dream. We also exercised to keep in fighting trim and talked over our limited options. As the days passed Armen and I began to become friends. I liked his easy manner and forthright ways. In no time we were plotting our escape. It might be obvious to all that escape was a hopeless pursuit, but such is the only recreation to those in prison.

I still held on to my .45, it was my one secret saving grace but I had limited ammunition. My captors had not taken it from me. I knew the weapon could do me no good while being locked away here in this cell. So Armen and I talked and decided, and we waited until the next time the guards came with our food. It was many nervous hours later when we were rewarded by hearing distant footsteps coming progressively closer to our cell.

Moments later our cell door was thrown open and armed guards entered, one of them throwing down two bowls of some disgusting mush at our feet.

"Eat!" the guard growled, then before he and his comrades knew what was happening, Armen and I were upon them. Our attack came as a complete surprise to the two most forward guards who had entered the darkness of our cell, our hands finding their throats and quickly snapping their necks. Then Armen and I together jumped the third and last guard, and that battle was over almost before it had begun.

Quickly Armen and I dressed in the guard's uniforms, taking their weapons and chain mail. Now, to all intents and purposes, we were men of Tar-Gool. Whatever that might mean.

Originally, I had wanted to escape Tar-Gool's dungeon as soon as possible to rescue Sirah, but something Armen had told me days before made me realize I had to amend my plans—as much as that infuriated me. For he had mentioned to me the knowledge and magical instruments the scientist had created. These could save the people of Ares and maybe eradicate the Winged-men menace forever. If it was possible, I had to give it a try. These devices might even help me save Sirah or get back to Earth. I had to see them. Armen was not agreeable at first. I knew I had to convince him to stick with me in my plan to reach Tar-Gool. Eventually he saw the reason in my plan and agreed. It had been the one crimp in us escaping from our cell sooner. For I realized that we had to find this Tar-Gool and discover all his scientific secrets for the good of the green people of Ares. I also realized that perhaps there might be some answer on how I had come to this strange world in the first place, from this mysterious scientist. He may hold the answers I needed.

* * * *

Once Armen and I escaped from our prison cell, we found ourselves in a long hallway with many similar cells. All were full of more helpless captives. They were a sorry looking lot and very scared. They would be set free now, for having taken the keys from our dead guards, Armen and I proceeded to liberate the entire population of Tar-Gool's dungeons.

Soon more than a hundred grateful and joyous men, most of them trained warriors, were ready to fight in defiance of Tar-Gool with us. Once Armen and I freed the men they kneeled to us in thankful obedience, pledging us their loyalty.

"Does anyone know where the armory is located?" I asked.

There was silence for a long moment, then one voice from the back spoke up, "Yes, I know. There is a guardroom at the top of that long series of steps. In there are many weapons. Swords. All that you need."

"All that *we* need," I corrected in a whisper.

I motioned for everyone to keep quiet and still, so as not to raise any alarm. I knew we had to move fast before more guards came, or discovered our escape. So I quietly led my small army up the stairs as we gingerly approached the guardroom.

We were about to rush into the chamber when I found that the massive door was locked from the inside. We were stymied.

A strange turn of events and totally unexpected. Had we been found out? It did not seem so, but I could not be sure. I kept the men quiet, with eyes peeled, then from below us I heard the unmistakable clang of swords and the fall of steel-shod boots.

We had been found out!

Tar-Gool's warriors came closer to us so quickly we found ourselves trapped upon the stairs, locked out of the armory with only three swords among us—the swords Armen and I had taken from our three cell guards. We stood there in fear, cursing our ill luck in dark whispers as we awaited our doom. I had some of the men doing all they could to try to break down the massive door of the armory before the soldiers captured us all.

Then Tar-Gool's warriors were upon us. It seemed they were as surprised to see us as we were to see them, but they were trained warriors and their commander was a sharp fellow who took in the scene all at once and knew what to do about it.

"The prisoners have escaped! Draw your swords and follow me!" and then he charged us with a hundred men at his back, all with drawn swords.

"Do not kill them! Capture them!" the commander ordered his men. "Tar-Gool needs subjects for his experiments!"

As the warriors charged up the stairs at us, I had no choice but to find some other way out.

I shouted to my men. "Quickly, come this way! Everyone, follow me!"

My group of escapees made a rapid run through the upper corridors of the halls of the rock-hewn fortress. We only had three swords between us at this point, and with the armory door locked to us we had no chance to obtain others. Unless our three swordsmen could win us more swords in battle. But that was a mighty hope. We were almost helpless and virtually unarmed, and we would all soon be dead or captured unless I found some way to save us.

I saw the tense look on the men's faces, from just moments before when they had been released from their cruel captivity, there had been real hope shining in their faces. Now there was a grim feeling of impending doom that you could actually smell seeping through the very pores of their skin. It was the smell of fear and death.

I led the enemy a merry chase throughout the vastness of the huge fortress. We ran with Tar-Gool's men at our heels, Armen, myself and one other man stopping from time to time to act as a rear guard. We did our best to fight off the advancing soldiers so that my men could get away, and did our best to impede the enemy from cutting down our unarmed men. The one thing that helped us most was the tight corridors, narrow hallways that made our defense much easier than I would have thought, so that our pursuers could only come at us two or three at a time.

Once we were able to gain a small lead, I discovered a particularly large and ornate hallway to the left. I lead my men down into this area. I noticed that Tar-Gool's warriors did not follow us there. I wondered why and began to get an ominous feeling. As it turned out I would soon find out that this was another mistake, for while entering the huge chamber did save my men from being massacred outright, or captured by Tar-Gool's soldiers, when we turned the corner my heart dropped for I saw the corridor ended a hundred feet ahead at a blank wall of solid rock.

Fear seized my valiant company of men now. We really did look to be doomed.

"I saw a large doorway back before the last turn," Armen shouted quickly. "Maybe we can hide in that chamber?"

I jumped at the opportunity and lead my men back to the chamber at a hearty run.

It became a race to see if we could reach the chamber door before Tar-Gool's warriors reached us with their swords.

The chamber must have been huge inside, for the outer doors alone were ten times the height of a tall man. My men pushed open the huge doors, which we thankfully found were unlocked, and we quickly entered the gargantuan hall. Behind us we saw Tar-Gool's soldiers advancing upon us. Soon they were but one hundred yards away. Once the last of our band entered the chamber we closed the huge metal doors behind us and locked them. I quickly ordered the men to grab up a large metal beam and put it into the brackets on each door to forestall Tar-Gool's warriors from entering. It would take them quite a while to break down those massive metal doors. We were safe for the moment and I allowed a deep breathe of relief as I took a quick inventory of our surroundings.

We found ourselves in a sparsely furnished hall. It was immense. I could see that at the far end of the room was an ornate throne high upon a raised dais. The throne was empty, as was the room. We walked on inside, closer to that throne.

Suddenly the walls on both sides were slid open as if they were on wheels, and we saw hundreds of armed warriors pour into the great hall taking up stations all around us. We were very neatly trapped. Within a few moments my men and I were completely surrounded by an armed and overpowering enemy.

"No resistance!" I ordered my men, unable to keep the frustration from my voice. For to resist now would have initiated a massacre of my unarmed comrades. I threw down my sword, and Armen did likewise. I raised my arms in surrender.

CHAPTER 8

IN THE CLUTCHES OF TAR-GOOL

We had no choice of course, so we threw down our three swords and whatever sticks and clubs my men had been able to gather along the way in our fight to use as weapons. We had no choice but to surrender. It was a humiliating and frustrating experience.

We were quickly lined up by the enemy troops, examined, inspected for knives and other hidden weapons. It seemed there were a few hidden weapons on some of my men. I smiled, they were brave fellows and would sell their lives dearly—if allowed to do so. We were lined up and told to wait. We waited. For what I knew not. Armen gave me a nudge in the ribs that brought my attention to someone entering the room.

I saw a small, wiry old man, an ancient green man, slowly walk over to the ornate throne in front of us and sit down. He watched me intently as I watched him.

Now an officer of the guard barked out a command, "All hail, Tar-Gool, Emperor of Ares!"

I was not aware Ares even had an emperor.

"Emperor of Ares, blah!" Armen whispered in defiance, but not too loudly, so that none could hear but I.

Nevertheless, Armen's words had been heard and he was quickly cuffed across the face by one of Tar-Gool's officers.

The officer warned in an almost robotic monotone, "Do not speak ill of our beloved Emperor! It is only through the magnificence beneficence and mercy of the Great Tar-Gool that you have not yet all been put to the sword!"

Armen stood tall, defiant.

I was shocked at the way the young officer had treated Armen, and that it seemed the officers and men under Tar-Gool obviously evidenced a loyalty to their master that seemed to border on fanaticism. It seemed incredible to me that they did so. I wondered why.

Our group of prisoners was bought forward. Tar-Gool motioned one of his officers to bring him a "volunteer" for an example of his powers. This was the same officer who had struck Armen, so without a word, he pointed his sword at my companion and then marched him before the throne where Tar-Gool sat so calmly—the self-stylized Emperor of Ares.

Tar-Gool appeared to be very old, even ancient, which for a green man on Ares meant he had to be over a thousand Earth years in age. A man his age was an incredible sight, a rare occurrence on this barbaric world where warfare took most of the men before they ever reached their first hundredth year in age, much less their first thousandth.

Now Armen stood before Tar-Gool, his warriors holding my friend firmly as a captive, as the old man looked down upon him with his sinister cold old eyes.

Tar-Gool was a strange looking old man, even for a green man. His body was small and obviously dehydrated, he was slim and dilapidated to the point of looking nothing more than some kind of animated human skeleton. The man appeared as if he were the very god of Death himself come back to life. It was a terrifying visage.

Tar-Gool was completely bald and hairless all over his body, and his face and skin was a sickly shade of blue-grey, even though he was a green man. That indicated he was prey to some serious disease. However, it was his eyes that held you most in their sway. Those amazing eyes! I shall never forget them! His eyes were red, blood red, a deep red fire, burning with the power of war and death and the will to destroy. I saw great power in those eyes, and maybe even wisdom.

It was Tar-Gool's deadly eyes that now bore down upon Armen. That look appeared more like some kind of examination or investigation, lasted for a few intense moments, and then to my surprise the guards that had been needed to hold Armen from resisting, simply released him. Armen just stood there serene and lackluster. I was shocked that he did not resist but what happened next shocked me even more. For the guards had not only released Armen, but they gave him back his sword. While I was completely surprised by what I had just seen, what was to come next, completely astonished me.

Knowing Armen's great hatred of Tar-Gool, I thought that right then and there—having the opportunity now—he might just make some bold attempt to kill our captor. Why Tar-Gool's officer had given Armen a sword I could not understand, but neither Tar-Gool, nor any of his men seemed the least bit troubled by this situation. I did not understand this at all. It seemed to bode ill for us all. I knew something very strange and inexplicable had taken place and as I looked closely upon my friend Armen, he did not seem to be the same person he had been scant moments before.

Then Armen pulled a complete about face in his manner and personality as I had grown to know it. I was astonished to see him get down on hands and knees in a submissive gesture to Tar-Gool. What came next stunned me, even as it had me reeling in surprise and rage.

"My beloved Emperor," Armen said without any seeming compunction, said in obvious sincerity, even joy, "I am Armen, King of the Sar Nomads. I am now honored to be your humble and obedient subject. I am yours to command, Master."

Well, I almost keeled over in shock and surprise at this, but it also put a cold chill throughout me. What had actually happened here? What had caused Armen to change so completely? So drastically! It was downright spooky!

Well, it was obvious what had happened. Somehow Tar-Gool had a way to control the minds of people. I was sure that those strange red eyes of his had something to do with his power. He was obviously some kind of mutant, and possessed incredible power over the minds of men and women. I realized now that he was an incredibly dangerous man.

Now Tar-Gool spoke once more and my thoughts and attention returned to the present and what was happening right before my eyes.

"Tell me, who was it who put you up to this revolt against my rule?" Tar-Gool asked Armen in a squeaky, high-pitched voice. "Who is your leader?"

"Most serene Highness," Armen answered, in a tone so differential and serious that it caused me to tremble with dread, wondering if the same mind control could be done to me. I knew that I would find out soon for Armen's next words sealed my doom. He pointed to me and said, "It is that man, the newcomer, Jon Kirk!"

I shook my head sadly. Stood my ground tall and proud.

Tar-Gool looked at me and smiled, he seemed delighted by my presence, "Yes! Yes, it is him! Quickly now! Bring Jon Kirk up here to me! Hurry, quickly now, so that he shall know true bliss as he becomes one of my most valued servants as one of my Converted Ones!"

I felt a chill that ran down into my very bones.

'Converted Ones?' I wondered what that might mean, but glancing at Armen and the blissful look upon his face, I grew very nervous for my future. Was that what Tar-Gool had done to Armen? Now I was scared of the same thing happening to me. Would I ever see Sirah again? Would I ever be able to save her from the Winged-men and the doom they planned for her? Oh, why had I not escaped this place when I had the chance! I realized that Armen, and all of Tar-Gool's warriors were nothing but slaves held in thrall by his powerful mind. And soon, I would be also.

Two armed guards now came for me.

I stood my ground with the hundred or so men in my small group of escaped prisoners who had not yet been Converted by Tar-Gool, but I could see that each and every one of them was terrified by what they had seen done to Armen. They were scared to death. I was horrified by what might happen to me. I stood besides some of the greatest green warriors of Ares and we trembled in our tracks at the thought of what was to be our fate.

I was lead towards the dais and throne where sat Tar-Gool, the self-styled Emperor of Ares. The idea of that loathsome creature up there controlling my mind made me boil over with rage and defiance. Would I ever be free once I had been Converted? What would happen to me once my mind was controlled by his mind? That is really what it was after all, mind control. And of course what was even more important to me at that moment was the thought that I would never see my lovely Sirah again, and not be able to come to her rescue.

That could not be allowed to happen while I still lived!

I was soon brought before the throne of Tar-Gool, and his terrible red eyes looked down upon me intensely. They were mesmerizing eyes. They truly bore down straight into your head, into your mind. I could feel the thoughts of the old man mixed with my own. His thoughts were becoming my thoughts. His words became my words, my thoughts, my desires. I could feel his mind entering my own, probing, speaking to me, forcing its will upon me. I fought back. I fought furiously and put up a wall that he could not breach. I was safe. He could not break through into my thoughts once I fought him. Soon I realized that his words and power were having no real effect. I could hear him, I could understand him, but while he commanded me—I was not forced to obey him! And I did not obey!

Yoooouuuu! Tar-Gool's mind whispered slowly within my own mind, *are now my slave. I-I am your m-master! Your only wish is to obey me!*

"Hah!" I shouted boldly defiant. "No way, old man!"

Tar-Gool tried to command me and I fought him back, building my wall against his mind higher and wider, so that he could not breach it no matter what he tried. And he tried every trick in his book of tricks and mind powers.

This went on for some time. After a while I felt myself growing weak and tired , but so was Tar-Gool. I hated the man more than ever now that I knew what he was really all about. For any man to have such terrible power, even if he could not work it on me, was devastating and vile. He was superhuman, but it was wrong what he was doing with his enormous gift and I told him so.

"You're wasting your time on me!" I shouted.

I do not know why his mind was not able to control mine. It must have been because I was not a green man like him, or that I was not of Ares, myself being an Earthman. Whatever the reason for my immunity of conversion through his mind powers, I secretly rejoiced at the fact. I was not under Tar-Gool's control. I was not controllable, not Converted. Yet I knew that Tar-Gool was sure that I had joined the ranks of his Converted Ones. I allowed him to believe I was under his control for the moment and acted the part. Believing I was one with him now, Tar-Gool even ordered that my sword, bayonet, and my fancy war club—my .45 Automatic—be returned to me.

"What sort of man are you, Jon Kirk? Where are you from?" Tar-Gool asked me carefully, showing deep curiosity. "Your skin, it is unlike the color of any true Ares men."

I decided to play the part of the willing slave for the time being, so I would tell him what he wanted to hear, and in the way he expected to hear it.

"My master," I said, trying not to choke or laugh at the very words as I spoke them, "I am from a faraway world, a planet in another star system."

He nodded for me to continue.

"Earth is very far from here," I added, stating the obvious, trying to buy myself some time.

At this response Tar-Gool rose and began to laugh and cry with apparent happiness. I was surprised by his joy and wondered what it could mean. Surely nothing good? For the first time since I had been in the presence of Tar-Gool, the old man actually smiled. I became even more nervous wondering just what the wily old creature was up to.

"Master?" I asked with suitable difference. "May I ask, why you are so happy?"

Tar-Gool continued with his twisted smile and then suddenly ordered every one out of the huge chamber except for myself. He even went so far as to order his personal bodyguard to be gathered up and to await him outside the chamber as well.

I was stunned, and in a few moments Tar-Gool and I were completely alone.

"Come closer, Jon Kirk," he asked, it was not an order or a command, but more of a request.

I nodded, and did as he had asked.

"Jon Kirk," he said in a low voice now, "I have something to tell you." He was so in control and so sane now, this did not seem to me to be the same Tar-Gool I had seen bare moments before. The madman was now gone. If he had truly ever existed. Now I really wondered just what Tar-Gool's game truly was.

Then he spoke up in a stronger voice, "Jon Kirk, I am a scientist. I am one of the last scientists in a great line of such men and women of the green race here on Ares. As you undoubtedly have discovered by now, science has been outlawed by the Zaran Winged scum that infest our world. I myself have been labeled an outlaw with a bounty put upon my head. Yet I live, and in fact, I thrive here in my secret fortress. For here I have power and the Zarans fear me. Many others on Ares fear me as well."

"They are wise to fear you, my lord," I said carefully.

He smiled. It was a smile that said he knew something that I did not know, but for the moment he was not going to tell it to me.

"Master," I asked softly, "how did I come here? And why?"

I realized that Tar-Gool knew much more than he had told me and that he and I were connected in some far deeper way I did not yet realize.

The little old man smiled again indulgently. Contemplatively. He was thinking and I grew nervous. I waited.

Tar-Gool suddenly smiled and said, "I have a certain transportation device which I invented in the old days. Simply put, I used it to grab you from your world and bring you here to my own."

This was a revelation to me, but I decided to keep mum for the moment. I nodded, knowing that what he said had to be true. Somehow. Super science now explained my advent upon the planet Ares. At least one of my many questions had been answered.

Tar-Gool looked at me closely and continued, "Understand, Jon Kirk, I was not aiming for you specifically. Any adult male warrior from your world would do. That is how you came to my world. As to how you came to be here in my fortress, you were in a battle and knocked out by a Zaran who brought you here and sold you to me."

"Yes," I recalled the battle with Zaor and the Warrior Caste against the Winged-men. "I still feel the bump on my head."

"The Zaran that carried you to me is one of a select few that work for me, they are under my control. They are difficult for me to command. He was wounded, so he dropped you to the ground. It was an unfortunate turn of events, for me. I assume for you as well. I lost control of you early on when you first set foot upon my world. However, you are fortunate that my winged agent was flying at a low level so you were not hurt when he dropped you. I imagine your additional weight, with the added weakness from his wound, had the effect of lowering his altitude. This is what saved your life when you fell. Afterwards, you were brought to me here."

"Have you brought others like me to this world, Master?"

"No," Tar-Gool replied with a sly smile. "None that lived. You are the first, John Kirk, and sadly the last. The machine I used to bring you here was very old, and the strain of transporting you here caused it much damage. Unfortunately, I do not have the time nor the knowledge, nor the special talent needed to repair this one or build another."

"So what is it you want of me?" I asked. "Why did you bring me to Ares? If you but tell me, Master, I am sure I can help you."

"Jon Kirk," Tar-Gool told me with a grim smile, "many people think I am an unkind old man, or even, a madman."

"I cannot believe that, Master," I told him, trying to keep a straight face and play along with what my part was supposed to be in our little conversation. Nevertheless, I could not resist a slight dig, so I told him, "Surely, that can not be?"

Tar-Gool laughed loudly at that and he eyed me suspiciously. Then he continued, "Some do say I am mad. And though it is not true, in one respect I must freely admit to a certain form of madness. For I am an old man, who yet lives for one reason, to see the Zaran Winged-men and all they represent destroyed and routed from my world."

I looked at the wizened old man before me and shook my head. Now I really was confused. Was this man actually some kind of Ares patriot? I was so astonished that I could not hide my feelings from him.

"Yes, Jon Kirk, I do care about my world and my people," he said proudly. Then he shocked me further when he told me, "and John Kirk, you can please stop acting now. I know that you have not become one of my Converted Ones."

I did not say a word for a long moment. I wondered how he knew, and what it now meant for me.

Tar-Gool smiled broadly, shrugged, said, "I am not the monster so many people think I am. You want to know how I know you are not under my control? I just know. It is as simple as that. I just know. I can tell these things, Jon Kirk."

I nodded grimly, I had been found out.

"Now what?" I said defiantly, "If you know I am not one of your damned Converted Ones, why did you go along with my charade and trust me alone here with you? I have my weapons now, I could easily kill you and escape."

"That is true, but you did not do that," he replied with confidence now. "I had to know for certain about you."

"So you tested me?" I asked.

"Yes," Tar-Gool replied simply.

"You risked much," I told him. "Why? What is your game and how do I fit into it?"

He shrugged, "Perhaps, I do risk much by being alone with you, but while I could not control your mind, I was able to look into it and see the type of man you are, Jon Kirk. You are a man of honor. A man of honor can always be trusted."

"I see. Tell me something. Why, if you hate the Winged-men as much as you say, do you not fight them?"

"I do, most definitely, Jon Kirk," Tar-Gool replied with a sharp tone. "But I do not have enough warriors to do so effectively. I also have to Convert many with my superior mind powers because I cannot command their loyalty. Unfortunately these days, many green warriors have become very mercenary fellows. Years ago, I was almost killed by my own bodyguard of green warriors, of all people. It shocked me to the core. They were found to be in the employ of agents for the Winged-men."

I looked at him and nodded, "The problems of leadership."

"Yes, so I had to do something about that situation. So I came up with a machine that changed my men into Converted Ones, which means that these warriors are entirely loyal to me. No one else. It is impossible for them to turn to treachery or to betray me. Even you must admit that in these treacherous times, such is a great boon in this conflict? However, Jon Kirk, you cause me much distress. You almost succeeded in freeing over a hundred prime warriors through your escape plan that I would have easily converted to my cause. Warriors that I need desperately to fight the Winged monsters. You see, the actual number of warriors I have converted to my cause is relatively small, mostly officers and my personal bodyguard. Even so, just doing this much, proves to be a great strain upon my mind. It takes great mental powers to convert these men and keep them under my control, even with the aid of my mind transmitter."

"Mind transmitter?" I asked carefully, for now he had named his machine and in naming it, its function as well.

"Yes, it is a machine, it boosts my mental powers," Tar-Gool explained simply.

I nodded, took a seat near Tar-Gool as we continued our discussion. How long we talked I did not know, but it was many hours. We talked of many things and asked each other many questions.

For his own effect, Tar-Gool was very forthcoming and seemed to be truthful in his responses to all my questions. I felt I should be as open with my replies. I soon began to take a far different opinion of the old man and took an actual liking to wily old Tar-Gool.

In one respect the old scientist was correct, the people of Ares were in dire fear of the Zaran masters, but since they were a constantly warring people, different groups would never successfully join together to expel the Zaran menace once and for all. The castes, tribes and clans were too divided and there was too much distrust.

Tar-Gool realized that one strong leader was needed to unite all the green peoples in a battle to defeat the Winged menace once and for all. Tar-Gool admitted to me that he was a rather helpless old man, even with his great brain power, and that the masses of diverse green people of Ares would never freely follow him in the coming battle with the Zarans. And even if they did, in time, there would be rivalry between the officers and kings, eventually treason and revolution in the ranks, or he would be assassinated by some treachery and all he had built up would be used for the benefit of one king and not the green people of Ares as he had intended. The Zarans would still be in power. Then the cause of freedom for the green people of Ares would be lost.

"You see, I do not trust my own people, Jon Kirk. I know them only too well."

"That is sad, I understand what you mean, but that is sad. A great leader, a truly great leader would do something to change that," I told him.

"Yes, Jon Kirk, but I am not that man." Then he looked at me closely, his penetrating gaze measuring me, "but can you be that man?"

"Me?" I asked surprised.

"Yes, of course, that is after all why I brought you to Ares."

I nodded, much of what he said made sense, but I did not see myself as the man for the job. I was not even a green man, I was not from Ares after all, but from Earth. No one would ever follow me, and I was not sure if I wanted them to. I only wanted to seek out my beloved Sirah and set her free. Then maybe return home to Earth.

One thing that was true, what he called 'The Cause' and Tar-Gool were one in the same. Intermingled so that I could not tell the two apart. In his efforts, Tar-Gool was merely doing what he thought best with the power he had in his possession.

I said, "You want to free the people of Ares and I agree with his noble goal, but I see it as ironic at the very least that your plan requires the enslavement of your people in order to free them."

Tar-Gool gave me a grim frown at these words. I could see he did not appreciate them, nevertheless they were true, and rather biting. I could see they gave him much food for thought.

* * * *

As the day passed, Tar-Gool talked more about his plans and my part in them. I could see that my biting words of the day before bothered him. That they did so spoke well for his true character, his innate nobility.

"As a scientist, I truly regret the use of the mind transmitter to control my people, but there will have to be many more Converted Ones if I am to build up an army large enough to effectively win Aresan freedom," he told me sincerely.

"Maybe some will need to be converted," I admitted, allowing him some leeway in the discussion. "However, many others such as Armen and his clan, should never have had their minds tampered with. They would have joined your cause willingly. They are natural allies, not enemies. They hate the Zarans. Allies are always more effective than slaves."

"Jon Kirk, you know how Armen fears and hates me," Tar-Gool replied. "I could not risk leaving him or his men uncontrolled in my midst."

"And me?" I asked outright, boldly. " What do you want me to do?"

Tar-Gool sighed deeply, tired now, "I am old, Jon Kirk, and no warrior. Soon I shall take the final voyage to meet my ancestors, and I welcome that day. In the meantime, I want you to lead my army of liberation. You can become that man. I want you to be the leader of the rebellion against the Winged-men and become of Emperor of Ares."

I sat there and looked at him amazed, unable to speak.

Tar-Gool continued, "I am in earnest. I shall stand at your side. I will help you all I am able. Difficult times such as these call for a young man, a gallant warrior, not an ancient creature like myself with one foot in the grave."

I was stunned by these remarks and told him so. I also told him that I was undeserving of his trust, much less the emperorship of the green peoples of Ares—not that it was his to give, I reminded him gently.

Tar-Gool laughed, but it was in good natured mirth. "There is no choice, Jon Kirk. You are the appointed one, the man from another world and the only man who can save my world. Please, I beg of you, you must accept this duty."

I must admit, even I thought Tar-Gool was quite mad then, but the more I thought it over, the more I realized that maybe his dream of freedom for the green peoples of Ares was within his power. It might just be possible.

One thing he was right about, the freedom fight needed a younger man to lead it, a warrior who had the strength and power to carry the battles to the enemy. I just did not see myself as that man.

Tar-Gool told me he wanted a good leader for his world to be in place in the event of his death, and he added carefully, "I have been watching you, Jon Kirk, ever since I brought you here to Ares. I have devices where I can see over great distances. It has been a test. A trial. I admit it. I am sorry but it was necessary, to know the true man, his true honor and integrity. And now, I am confident that you are the one man who can lead this sad world to freedom. So please, do not deny this last wish of a dying old man to see his people free."

I nodded, but kept silent for the moment. I didn't know what to say to him about all this, but I knew what I had to do.

* * * *

For many weeks I stayed with Tar-Gool and helped him in his preparations—or he helped me in mine. I made sure that Armen was immediately de-converted and now he and all Tar-Gool's men had their free will back. After I explained everything to Armen and the other warriors, they were all eager to join our cause.

Armen, Tar-Gool and myself ended up working closely to-gether, and soon the three of us became fast friends. Armen and I became especially fond of old Tar-Gool, which surprised both of us considering our first dealings with him. He was an old coot, but not without mercy and compassion, and he dearly cared for his people—he had just gone about helping them in the wrong way. He admitted that now he had been wrong and was sorry for his earlier mistakes controlling the minds of his warriors. Now that the men knew what he was trying to accomplish, we were all behind him, and that made him realize the extent of his folly. He was sorry but he was just so cantankerous. The fight for freedom was his mission in life and he did not want to fail the people of Ares.

As time passed we met with other leaders of the green peoples who joined our cause, including Sahn Jor, who was the king of the Caste of Woodworkers. He had been a friend of Tar-Gool for many years and had also been unconverted by the master scientist. He assured us that his people would fight for our cause if Tar-Gool and I lead the fight. I assured him that we would.

In those frantic weeks of arming and planning, freedom became the byword, as all of Tar-Gool's men were now unconverted due to my urgings, and now had their free will back, but with their free will came their true personalities and often prejudices. The good and the bad. Tar-Gool had relented in his control and now saw the error of his logic, and the irony of leading a righteous cause for freedom by enslaving to his cause the very people he wanted to set free. Many of these warriors joined us eagerly once they were told the truth, but there were a few who were still fearful of the Zaran winged menace, and they did not much trust Tar-Gool. I could not disagree with them but I did try to convince them to join our cause. Every one of these men had felt Zaran oppression in their lives, they hated the Winged-men, but they were terrified of them as well.

The worse thing to deal with were the various clan and caste rivalries and old feud hatreds. These old hatreds had to be put to bed, buried deeply, but it was not easy.

It was times like these when I often thought of Sirah. I was determined that I would go and find her soon. Then set her free. The only thing that was stopping me was that Tar-Gool assured me Sirah could only have been taken to one location, the city of Caliat to the south.

"She will be safe for some months, Jon Kirk," the old scientist told me with open fatherly sympathy. "Fear not, you shall get to her in time. The Zarans do not use their slaves until they have been well fed, they keep them for many months, sometimes even years before…

"Before they eat them!" I growled in rage.

"Yes, I am sorry, but you still have time, we have time, let us make the most of it."

"Where is this city?" I asked, straining to hold my anger in check.

Then Tar-Gool gave me a very basic geography lesson about the planet Ares. He told me the single land mass on Ares is called Cos and it is divided into six sections, or Zaran provinces, each with one of the six Zaran cities as the capital. These six cities control the planet and all of them pay tribute to Zar, the capitol city where the emperor of the Winged-men reigns. So it was Caliat that I made our plans to attack first. It took time and much preparation. Tar-Gool assured me that Caliat would be a tough nut to crack.

As the days passed I became increasingly anxious and fearful for Sirah's safety, but we had to strengthen our forces before we could move against the enemy or save her. We had sent out riders and messengers to the four corners of the continent, and now many others joined in our quest for freedom. For most of the green people of Ares their hatred of the Winged-men far outweighed their fear of them. So we planned the attack and sacking of the enemy city of Caliat.

Other leaders, of various castes, clans and tribes now joined our cause. Besides Tar-Gool, myself, Armen, and Sahn Jor, there were Crooch and Tavan of the Southern Farmers who now joined us bringing many men with them. By now not one man remained under Tar-Gool's mind control and the men and their swords were dedicated to our cause.

Tavan and his people promised to do everything in their power to help our cause as well, but Crooch seemed a different story. To me, Tavan and Crooch, the two leaders of the farming castes seemed to be as different as night and day. Crooch would complain and argue constantly with almost everyone. He questioned orders, always seemed to have an excuse for any problem, but his excuses always seemed plausible. Tavan would tell us that his people were simple farmers, and not trained warriors, which was true, but he noted that if Sahn Jor and his Woodworkers could fight, then his people could do no less. Tavan seemed to be a good man, a man of honor, he was well liked and respected by all. He was correct of course, his people were not trained warriors. That was the problem. What we needed were trained warriors. An entire army of them.

What I wanted was to have the entire Caste of Warriors, all of the various tribes and clans join our cause. However, with me away from their mountain sanctuary here with Tar-Gool, and Zaor apparently dead now, Tob was still the king and apparently ruled unopposed. I knew that he would never help us in our cause. In fact, Tob would surely kill me if he ever had the opportunity. Just as surely as I would him. Maybe he would even make some treacherous bargain with the Winged-men? I felt that anything was possible with such a man—a man who possessed no honor at all.

It was not long before many other warrior leaders joined our group of freedom fighters in support of our cause. We were happy to receive the support of Vakon of another Southern Farmer clan, and Ogz, leader of the fierce Vaki Nomads; both of which were great rivals of Armen's tribe. They were persuaded to join us and to work together for the good of the cause. For the most part, they did. So things seemed to be running smoothly with all the disparate groups. I noticed that even Vakon and Crooch seemed to be getting along better.

As the days passed into weeks our group became a formidable force, a free association of warriors and tradesmen working together for the freedom of the green people of Ares. However, with the addition of Ogz and Vakon we began to have some problems. Arguments, jealousy in the ranks, power struggles among the various commanders, old rivalries and hatreds abounded. There was distrust. Sometimes I almost wished old Tar-Gool still had these men under his mind control to keep them silent and cooperating. When I stated that in anger during one meeting, that seemed to cause everyone to cool off a bit, at least temporarily. I knew tensions were rising as we got closer to the date when we would set forth in battle. I could feel the stress, the anxious feelings of impending war in the air.

Nevertheless, the one thing that Tar-Gool in his great wisdom had always feared seemed to be coming true. Dissension and rivalry seemed to be growing as we got closer to our date of action, and it was growing because there was no action for our forces yet.

The men were growing increasingly restless. So was I. I thought of Sirah and chaffed at every day I waited and wasted, but I knew our force had to be ready before I set it lose.

I once again urged for attack, but Tar-Gool said we were not ready yet.

"Well when will we be ready!" I argued hotly, seeking action.

"Be patient, Jon Kirk," Tar-Gool told me softly. "Soon. Soon, my friend."

I nodded, he was correct after all, but it was galling to wait for so many weeks.

Things took an ugly turn with Crooch, who with his friend and fellow countryman, Vakon, began to argue and threaten on almost every subject unless they got their way. They were like children, and I told them so, but that only made matters worse. It almost came to a blood duel, but Armen stepped in between us, and his cooler head wisely told us, "You should spill Winged-men blood, not each others!"

That cooled us all down for a day.

Nevertheless, it seemed to me that Crooch and Vakon had no serious care for our cause at all now, if they ever had in the first place. I began to wonder about them. Was I just letting the dissension and rivalry get to me? Was I just becoming suspicious? Or did I really have something to be suspicious about with these two?

I asked Tar-Gool about it, "You are tense, eager to fight, so are they, so are we all. Once the battle begins, Jon Kirk, all this turmoil will melt away."

I nodded, the old scientist was wise, Armen also agreed with his words, so I dropped my suspicions.

Well, Crooch and Vakon did not relent in their talking, their scheming. I spotted them many times whispering furtively between themselves when they thought no one was around, as if they were in some treacherous plan. Was I just being suspicious? Maybe paranoid? I admit my dislike for both men. I did not trust them and I felt they had no honor. But was I being unfair to them? After all, they were not warriors, they were simple men, and they had bravely joined our cause. I realized that I had no real evidence against them and let the matter drop. We were getting close to the attack date and I had more weighty matters upon my mind.

It was old Tar-Gool, who was a better judge of Ares nature than I, who now had become a suspicious old coot, "I see the seeds of treachery being sown here, Jon Kirk."

"But you told me...?"

"I know what I said days ago, but I have been watching them as well. I do not like what I see. I do not trust them," Tar-Gool told me one evening.

I nodded, he was probably right, and I told him I felt the same way, but there was no actual evidence against these men. They had done nothing to warrant any action on my part. Talking, even in whispers, was no crime, and I did not want to lead any such army of men where that kind of suspicion caused problems where there might not be any. I knew the score with them, I would watch them, but it was a waiting game.

However, as we came closer to the day of attack, the problem with Vakon and Crooch grew so bad that it even affected my best and most trusted lieutenants, Armen and Ogz. These two men began to have a go at each other, with arguments and cursing that threatened to lead to blows. It got to the point that neither man could stand to be seated at the same table. It was a bad omen. By themselves, each man was easy to get along with, and they were each true friends to me and the Cause—as well as valued officers. I told them this and each man acknowledged the truth of it, but nothing came of my words to make them get along. It got so bad I had to separate them and meet with each one by himself out of the vision and hearing of the other. It was becoming unbearable and a serious impediment to my command.

Then there was the hatred of the Vaki clan against the Sar clan. It was so very well known that I should have realized that Ogz and Armen could not stop the rivalry even had they wanted to do so. So busy were Tar-Gool and I in those last days before the attack on Caliat, and dealing with the Armen and Ogz problem, I gave little notice to the now quiet and silent actions of Crooch and Vakon. I should have known that once those two vipers grew silent, treachery could not be far behind. It proved a drastic mistake for me. The two men now hardly ever came to staff meetings and I tended to forget about them, secretly wishing they would run off and dessert, but they did not leave and only continued their scheming behind my back.

By this time Sahn Jor and Tavan were eager to leave Tar-Gool's fortress and get back to their lands to arouse their people for the coming fight. I sent them on that mission and hoped they would rally many of their men to our cause.

It was difficult those last few days at Tar-Gool's fortress. Armen and the Sar Clan and Ogz and his Vaki Clan now refused to have their men even fight alongside each other in the storming of Caliat. I could not believe this situation. Tar-Gool and I argued with them incessantly to work together for victory. Eventually I had to agree to do a last minute reorganization of my battle plan, to separate their hosts. I had to ensure that, horror of horrors, the men of these two groups would not decide to fall upon each other instead of the Winged-men! Tar-Gool and I saw our fine plans seem to melt away right before our eyes with all these problems, and day by day I saw Caliat and Sirah getting farther away from me.

CHAPTER 9

THE TREACHERY OF CROOCH

After much wine and pressured words I finally convinced Armen to join his force together in our battle plan with the Vakis of Ogz. I once again tried to convince Tar-Gool that we needed an immediate attack on the city of Caliat.

"Our entire army will fall apart unless we use it soon," I pleaded. "These men are restless, they are at each others throats now. I don't know how long I can hold them all together."

Tar-Gool nodded, "Yes, Jon Kirk, I believe you are correct. It is now time."

I sighed with relief. Now we were ready. For now Tar-Gool had given me the green light to lead the attack on Caliat. The wait had proved useful for the men were well trained now and ready for victory. It was a great accomplishment to bring this mass of unruly and undisciplined men together and hold them together for this long, and all things considered I was duly proud. I would be even more proud when I saw that army fighting; killing Winged-men, sacking Caliat, and then enabling me to free my beloved Sirah.

I was about to command the various tribes and clans and order them to begin their march when a young warrior in Tar-Gool's bodyguard hastily came over to me.

"Jon Kirk!" he cried, holding back on a rage that I could see plainly in his face now. "That treacherous one, Crooch, and his sly ally, Vakon, have escaped! I do not know how long they have been missing, but Tar-Gool told me to tell you that he is sure that they have betrayed us."

"Betrayed us to the Winged-men?" I asked carefully, growing furious quickly, hoping it was not true. Perhaps the men had only deserted to go back home? Or so I hoped.

The warrior only nodded fearfully.

"So be it!" I growled and left the chamber.

I immediately met with Tar-Gool and Sahn Jor to discover more information about this dark turn of events. I learned from many witnesses a good picture of what had transpired. It seemed the two men had stolen away in the middle of the previous evening like thieves in the night. Thieves in fact who we were sure now had stolen our plans for the attack on Caliat. Of course we ordered searchers in all the caverns and caves, and all the buildings of Tar-Gool's fortress were searched from top to bottom. But there was no sign or Crooch and Vakon. They were gone. There were also missing plans of the attack on Caliat. They had all disappeared.

"Probably just as well about them being gone," Sahn Jor said ruefully. There was no love lost between him and those two. "They were only troublemakers anyway. The missing plans are the real problem."

"Yes, I agree," I stammered holding down my anger. When I caught those men…! "I am glad they are gone. The plans will have to be changed now, of course. It galls me the plans are known by our enemies, but perhaps we can use this to our advantage."

"How so?" Tar-Gool asked, he was crushed by the treachery, something he had always feared might hinder our cause. The old man looked tired now, worn out with worry and fear, fear that we might not succeed in our mission to free the green people of Ares.

I nodded, said, "Now we have no choice, we must move up our attack on Caliat. We have to go with the forces and men we have in hand, and we must attack right away before the Winged-men can be notified and fortify the city."

I immediately gave the word for our army to begin our advance. That morning thousands of warriors and armed men began the march on Caliat. I coordinated the march, as spies and scouting parties I had sent out days before began to report back to me with various bits of valuable information. The news, they came back with however, was not good.

"It may be impossible for us to take Caliat, Jon Kirk," my lead scout told me that morning. "There are over fifty thousand winged warriors within the city. These are trained, hardened warriors, vicious flying monsters who will have a tremendous advantage over our ground troops. Another advantage for the Zarans is that they hold that city securely, and our troops will have to dislodge them. We will have to breach the walls. Enter the city. Not an easy task."

"Nothing worthwhile is easy, my friend," I told the scout. "Go and get your men ready."

At this grim news Tar-Gool became thoughtful. Was he having second thoughts about moving our forces now? I listened to his wise words with regret. He did not want to waste our valiant forces in a useless attack, nor bleed our men in some hopeless massacre. I agreed. I realized that there was nothing left to do but for me to go to Caliat myself and ascertain the true situation in that city and what could be done about it. Because one way or another, I was going to bring this army to the walls of Caliat, and Caliat was going to fall!

My plan for war was set. I had more than a hundred thousand warriors from all the various tribes and castes now ready and eager to draw their swords and kill Zarans. I knew our agents in the city of Caliat would rouse the green people who were slaves to begin their revolt when they received our word to do so. We had seen to it that weapons had been smuggled into the city over the last few weeks just for this revolt. Our men had been training with swords day and night. We had planned well. We were ready for battle.

I knew the Zaran Winged-men were a formidable enemy, but they were also an enigma. Nothing much was actually known about them or their society, for the green slaves never left the Zaran cities alive to tell anything of what they had observed there. Only wild rumors abounded, most were not trustworthy. A few select green men who were merchants were allowed outside a Zaran city, but they could not enter any city upon pain of death. So they must do their trading business outside the city at the main gate among the green slaves sent by their Zaran masters. This is also how we sent spies into Caliat. While no one was able to escape the city, the Zarans never imagined that green men would actually seek to willingly enter their cities.

The information these spies brought back to us was priceless and it told another story. There was trouble in Caliat among the various Zaran factions and the king. The green slaves were full of rage and ready to revolt. They were armed and eager to kill their Zaran masters, only awaiting our word to begin the slaughter. For there was no doubt that a slaughter I was sure it would become.

THE WINGED MEN | 71

However, that did not phase me at the moment. I did not concern myself with Zaran dead. There was more to consider. I learned that there was a general lack of discipline and overconfidence among the Zaran troops as well. By now they had heard of an impending attack, but their leaders did not actually believe it would ever come to pass. They openly scoffed at it, in fact. And if it came to pass, the Zarans were more than confident their swords and their power of flight would win the day for them against the green men as it always had done.

There is an old Ares myth from long ago. It was something that Tar-Gool and many of the green people of his world believe to be true. It says that there are no female Zarans on the planet Ares. It tells the story that Zaran reproduction is accomplished by Zaran males mating with captive green female salves. I shuddered at this incredible and horrifying news. Could it be true? I prayed that it was not. Obviously the females involved in this atrocity had no choice in the matter. Their only recourse to this vile action was to seek self-destruction before the deed was done. I learned that many female green women who were slaves resorted to suicide rather than submit to the enemy in this fashion. It is said the suicide of green female slaves now happened in ever increasing numbers and in ever innovative ways.

Tar-Gool told me, "It seems the male Zaran gene is always dominant, so that a Zaran Winged-man mated to a green female, always produces a Zaran male offspring."

I nodded, this grim news was making me sick and angry. I felt so helpless to protect Sirah. "So what happens to the mothers?'

Tar-Gool shook his head sadly, "It is said they are killed immediately after the birth of the new winglet—then eaten by the father and child in some kind of ritual meal."

I shuddered at this news and Tar-Gool gave me a sad look that could not hide his sense of doom.

"Why are you telling me this now?" I asked the old Ares scientist. "Are you telling it to me just to be cruel, just to torture me? There is nothing I can do about any of it while I am here."

Tar-Gool looked dreamy-eyed. "I know of your love for Sirah, Jon Kirk, I just want you to know that, even now, it may be too late to save her. I did not want to give you false hope. I did not want to tell you this sooner because I feared you would torture yourself with things not under your control. This is the way things are done here on Ares. You must accept that reality. If it is so, it is so."

"Well I do not accept that reality, Tar-Gool!"

He smiled, "Then change it, Jon Kirk! Change this world for the better!"

"I will!"

That night I decided upon my plan. I would get an early start first thing the next morning and head out to Caliat with a small force of Sar scouts. I dreamed how we would roam the flat plains and dry deserts of Ares on our way to the Zaran city. My thoughts were full of sweet dreams of finally finding Sirah and setting her free, but at the end of each dream I saw visions of fierce winged warriors coming at me with blood-drenched swords.

* * * *

Crooch and Vakon had been gone two days when their true treachery became apparent to us. We had assumed they were up to no good, but it wasn't until that night that what they had done became clear. That night Crooch and Vakon returned to Tar-Gool's fortress, and they returned with half a hundred winged warriors and stormed the fortress and caves of Tar-Gool. They did not come to make war, their raiding party was not that large. They came to capture the leaders of our plot. They came after Tar-Gool, myself, and the others of our commanders. It was a smart move for them.

The Winged-men swooped down upon the roof of Tar-Gool's fortress silently and quickly disposing of our guards. Their attack was totally unexpected. Their presence went unnoticed. They quickly made their way down into the fortress to the officer's quarters. Crooch and Vakon, the vile traitors, lead them, showing the invaders the way to their prize.

At the officer's quarters it was our great luck that all were absent except for myself who was fast asleep, having gone to bed early that night to be well-rested for my early morning's travel to Caliat.

As it turned out, I didn't have to go to Caliat at all, for it now seemed that Caliat had come to me!

The invaders were on me in an instant. Before I even knew what happened, I found myself a prisoner once more. Half a dozen of the savage winged horrors were upon me, and I found myself quickly tied up and gagged. In the doorway I saw Crooch and Vakon smiling as they looked at me now helplessly bound. They had what they had come for. They had the leader of the freedom fighters now as their prisoner. They had me trussed up and in their power.

I was quickly brought up to the roof of the fortress and then held there for some time. I vaguely wondered what they were waiting for; why they had not become airborne. Then I saw what it was that had stalled their departure. Crooch and Vakon were waiting to capture, or murder, Tar-Gool. They were also planning to have their Zaran allies murder as many of our officers as possible in an effort to destroy our leadership. It was a bold and vicious plan. Crooch and Vakon had sold their honor and our lives to the Winged-men of Caliat for gold and silver.

I struggled in my bonds but was unable to get free. I felt defeated and helpless, but my anger and rage at what had been done would not allow me to give up. I still lived, and I have always believed that while there is life there is always hope for victory.

It was not long before I heard the sounds of fighting from below me in the lower chambers. The loud clang of swords, fierce screams and howls, the curses of fighting men, and the cries of the dying. It all came plainly to my ears now as I lay their bound and helpless. I yearned to be a part of it. I yearned to let Crooch and Vakon, and their winged allies, taste my blade. A blade hungry for their blood. But it was not to be. I was a prisoner now, helpless and unable to do anything but watch what was going on around me in doomed silence.

Then I saw the invaders bring out a small bald-headed figure that was also tied and gagged, much as I was. Following them were Crooch and Vakon. I knew this must be Tar-Gool who they had kidnapped and now held prisoner. So now he was captured as I was. My thoughts instantly flew to my companions; Armen, Ogz, Sahn Jor and Tavan. Where were they? Were they now all dead? I only hoped that they were leading Tar-Gool's troops to our rescue. I even allowed myself the fleeting hope that they would soon break though the ranks of the winged invaders who made a wall around us. Then I saw Crooch speak to the Zaran commander.

"It is time. We have what your master wanted," Crooch said triumphantly.

"Yes, you have done your job well. There will be much gold for you for serving those from Zar so well," the enemy commander told Crooch.

The battle was over. Our rescue force had not yet reached the roof. Suddenly Tar-Gool and I were grasped by the Zaran monsters and carried aloft in winged flight by our captors presumably toward the enemy stronghold city of Caliat.

We were in the air in an instant. The Winged-men flew high and fast. Soon the fortress of Tar-Gool was only a tiny speck on a receding horizon and the mountains were gradually disappearing in the distance.

After many hours of flight we came to a large plain at the end of which was a vast expanse of the coastline of the only land mass of Ares. We followed this for a time southward, toward Caliat.

As we flew toward Caliat, carried by our winged captors, I chanced to see Crooch in the group carried aloft by another Zaran. He was smiling evilly when he saw me, very satisfied with himself and his deed, mocking me with his dark laughter and harsh words. Vakon joined him, and then all their winged allies joined in.

Tar-Gool and I made eye contact. We did not lament, nor cry. We thought and planned. We would have our revenge. We still lived!

CHAPTER 10

ABDUCTED BY THE WINGED-MEN

It was not many hours later that the Zaran city of Caliat became visible to us in the distance. I was surprised, for the city seemed beautiful beyond belief, and it actually glowed of gold and silver in the bright red sun light. It was a sight to behold.

As we flew closer I noted many well formed and gorgeous buildings of various designs each one thoroughly enhancing the beauty of Caliat. It seemed strange to me that the barbarous Winged-men would choose to live in such a lovely city, for art and beauty to them were looked upon as nothing but weakness. They had no interest in such things. I knew that such loathsome creatures could never have built a shining city like Caliat.

Of course, I was soon to learn that Caliat was one of the oldest cities on Ares, having been built by the ancient green race long before the Zarans ever came and conquered the planet. Also, the city had been the Zarans' most recent conquest, having been the last and most glorious city of the green people to hold out against the Winged-men over a thousand years ago.

This was the city that Tar-Gool's ancestors had come from and had ruled over. The city they hard created. This was the glorious city of Caliat. Now not so glorious and under enemy occupation. Tar-Gool constantly spoke of the glory of the past people from this city, before the dark blight of the Zarans had come and destroyed everything here and all over Ares. It was before an entire world of green humans had been enslaved, or made outlaws on their own planet.

Now I realized why, that when I had first met Tar-Gool he had referred to himself as the Emperor of Ares. For in truth he was a direct descendent from that last green emperor of shining Caliat before the beastly Zarans overran the city. And I could not think of a better man, nor a more patriotic devotee to Ares freedom than Tar-Gool to bear that honorary title. However, sensing his impending death through old age, Tar-Gool now wished that I would take that title when he passed on. When I had asked him why he wanted me to take that burden, he told me that he had his own special reason, but he mysteriously said that he could not tell me as yet. I remained perplexed.

As we came closer to Caliat I now could notice that the Zarans had ruined much of the great old city. Neglect and decay was the results of their reign. The city lay in ruins. However, much of it's ancient glory and grace were still evident. It was sad to see what had once been, and then what was left now under Zaran rule, even though one could see the remains of what once had been a magnificent city. Caliat had been truly a city befitting an emperor.

Soon we were flying right over the huge city center and I noticed Winged-men everywhere. I also saw large numbers of green men and women, all slaves working under the cruel whips of fellow greens, traitors who were now overseers for their Zaran masters. My blood boiled to see this. To see green men who had become traitors to their own people and now worked for the hated enemy was a most vile offense to my eyes.

I would later find out that the Zarans actually did no work at all. They busied themselves only with war and hunting, eating and killing, looting and torture. It is said the Zarans are expert torturers. I could well believe that to be true.

It seemed that this was to be my only fate at the hands of the Winged-men now that I had been captured by them. I would have to make sure if I was ever given a chance, I would sell my life dearly and take as many of the enemy with me to the Afterworld as possible.

Minutes later we landed on the roof of a large and impressive structure. It was an enormous building, obviously a palace of some kind. Quickly we were let down, untied, and with sword points pressed strategically at our backs, Tar-Gool and I were lead under heavy escort down a stairway and into the bowels of the great building. It was Crooch who informed us that this was the royal palace of the Zaran ruler of Caliat. I had expected as much and readied myself for new betrayals.

We walked through a long unkempt companionway which showed massive signs of deterioration, as with everything the Zarans seemed to touch or control. They were by nature arrogant and lazy brutes, but deadly dangerous.

Soon we were lead into the Great Hall of Pondinan, the Zaran King of Caliat. I remembered that of the six Zaran cities, each one had their own king, while at the main capital at Zar, was where their overall leader, the imperial emperor ruled. The imperial emperor at Zar ruled over all the Zaran winged creatures, but over each of the individual cities the six kings ruled as they desired, only showing fealty to the imperial emperor at Zar.

We were roughly lead to a section of the room under heavy guard. Presently Pondonan came into the chamber escorted by his bodyguard and sat before us with his advisors and generals. The Caliatian ruler was an old and obviously weak winged brute. He seemed in ill health, and if I had anything to do with it, he would be in worse health before this audience was over. He was perhaps as old as Tar-Gool himself, yet he was almost completely bald and hairless, just one wisp-thin shank of hair atop his head. It was strange for a Zarian, even an old one. Pondonan's wings were also different. Unlike the usual rich dark color of most of his people, his wings were a dark flat black and looked lifeless. They looked old and unusable. I doubted he had the energy to fly any longer.

"So...?" Pondonan said thoughtfully, mouth pursing his words carefully, "what am I to do with you?"

"Release us immediately," I said bluntly, seriously.

Pondonan shook his head, allowed an evil leer, "You two are the leaders of this revolt against me and the Zaran race."

Tar-Gool and I did not reply.

Pondonan just laughed, enjoying his power and seemingly victory over us, while his courtiers and staff turned grim and terrifying evil grins upon us. It was a grim assemblage that boded deadly for Tar-Gool and myself. However, I did notice one younger Zaran of interest, who sat next to the king on a lower throne. This, I thought, must certainly be the king's son.

"Great King," this younger Zaran, who we later learned was indeed the king's son, named Prince Orton, said boldly, "you should kill these creatures at once."

I looked grimly at Tar-Gool. This young prince did not mince words, but he was smart and knew a danger when he saw it. If I ever became free, I would do all I could to bring down the Zaran rule here, and in the doing there would be hell to pay for the enemy at my hands.

"No, my son," and I was shocked when the old king brutally struck his son's face right there in front of us and the entire court. It was a most brutal reaction to the young Prince's words and totally unprovoked. I saw that the old king had some considerable strength left, for he sent his son sprawling at our feet. Not one person in that chamber lifted a hand to help the young prince. The brutality of the event shocked me.

Prince Orton got to his feet slowly, his usually purple face now a darker black and red with rage in the Zaran manner of intense anger and embarrassment. I notice that his hand was at the hilt of his sword, but just at that moment a winged warrior beside the king let out a grim laugh at Orton's misfortune. That was enough. It had only been a small laugh, barely heard, but heard nonetheless. Its maker soon lay dead, as Prince Orton exploded in a sudden fit of rage, drew his sword and quickly pieced the warrior's heart before the man even knew what had happened. We all gathered that Prince Orton would have loved to do the exact same thing to his father, the king, but wisely thought better of that. At least for now. There was no love lost between this father and son, that was obvious. It seemed to be the Zaran way, force and brutality were their mannerisms accented by killing and torture. Violence and death were a way of life to them. They were cruel vicious creatures that did not deserve to exist.

Then I watched in awe as Prince Orton bent down to the dead warrior and calmly proceeded to cut off the warrior's wings.

"This one insulted me and will be used to feed the cattle," Orton growled in dire menace. "Anyone else here wish to feed the cattle? They are in need of much food!"

I was to find out later that by the word "cattle," Orton meant the green people who were slaves. It seemed that it was the height of insult for any Zaran to be used as slave food, especially since the slaves were used as the main staple of food for the Zarans. It was a heinous insult. We could see the fear in everyone's eyes as Prince

Orton looked at each and every one of his countrymen, and then his gaze rested defiantly upon his father, the king.

I was greatly shocked by the cruelness of the Winged-men, yet Tar-Gool who stood quietly beside me showed no surprise at all. I think he rather expected it. He knew them a lot better than I did.

"You must know," Pondonan said to Tar-Gool and I smugly, ignoring his son for the moment, "that your army, without you two to lead it, will fall apart just as every other expedition lead by the greens has come against us here. Your men would rather fall upon each other than dare attack a Zaran stronghold city such as Caliat. You have no hope of victory." He then laughed in my face, for he saw our task was impossible. All his courtiers and men at arms enjoyed the joke and laughed along with him.

Tar-Gool and I stood silent and bided our time, which I felt was running out much too quickly. I had to come up with something to save us—and soon!

Pondonan loudly proclaimed, "Never has a Zaran city fallen to the green cattle. The greens are only fit to be cattle, and this city shall remain ours forever. You were fools even to plan such a venture. I acknowledge you both have great ambition, but for lowly creatures such as yourselves, that kind of ambition can only be rewarded by a slow and painful death."

Well, there it was, the death sentence. Tar-Gool and I had expected as such and we were not surprised. We had spoken of this possibility when making our plans. We had both agreed that if it ever came to this we would sell our lives dearly, taking as many of the enemy with us to the land of the Afterworld as we were able. I looked at Tar-Gool and gave him the sign, and he nodded that he understood and was ready.

Then suddenly before we could act, from the opening in the ceiling above, a Zaran warrior flew down into the huge chamber. He landed quickly, bowed, saluted Pondonan and then spoke, "Great King, I am a captain of the 4th Korvanth Scouting Corps. I was on a mission to the Coastal Mountains when I came upon a great number of green troops massing together. They are Ares green men, my Lord! Reports from the southern regions also indicate that…"

That was the last word that warrior spoke for at that moment fighting began to break out as Tar-Gool and I lifted swords from our guards and proceeded to cut down surprised Winged-men as fast as we were able. No one there had expected such a bold move from mere cattle. Both of us were more than able swordsmen. We cut and slashed the shocked enemy before they even were able to draw their own swords and we took down over a dozen. It was a most exhilarating attack, our blades sang fast and sure, but never fast enough for Tar-Gool and me.

I hacked down three winged Zarans before they knew what was happening and soon I was fighting my way toward the throne and the king. I saw that on the other side of the room Tar-Gool was doing the same. We caused utter devastation and chaos in that room. The old man turned out to be an excellent swordsman, quick and quite spry, so that he had little trouble in defeating the large lumbering and slow Zaran monsters—a race of creatures that while excellent killers, were not very good swordsmen. They also proved to be not as nimble fighters on the ground as when they were flying in the air, where they held a natural advantage. Tar-Gool quickly dispatched his fourth victim and I fell my sixth with my point cutting out a gash across his throat.

Then my sword slashed into my next victim, sending him sprawling down to the floor in pain and I found that now the way was open for me to reach the Zaran king.

Should I dare it?

Yes I would dare!

Soon I was face to face with Pondonan himself. He was frozen in terror and surprise by my presence and my sword, surely nothing like this had ever happened to him before. It could not be happening! But it was! He drew his weapon and came at me and I met him in a grand charge that turned into a grand battle at the foot of his throne.

"You should have listened to your son!" I shouted to him as we brawled back and forth with thrashing swords, metal scraping and hitting metal. He was not a bad swordsmen but no real challenge to me. I was soon able to cut him on the shoulder and he cried out in pain and rage.

"You shall be dead in the most terrible manner I can devise for assaulting the royal personage of the king!" His Majesty shouted at me in rage and terror, but even as he voiced these threats I think that he knew the truth. He was no match for me in battle. The

THE WINGED MEN | 81

Zaran king was able enough, for a Winged-man, but not a very good swordsmen, so that for me the battle with him soon became bloody murder. I was not upset by the situation, for it is nothing less than he and his people deserved. I struck fast and true, giving him the mercy of a quick death. Pondonan soon lay in a pool of his own blood at the foot of his throne.

Tar-Gool and I now came together, fighting back to back against our enemies so as to leave no opening for their blades. Many of the Zarans had run off. Those left were very leery of us. However, the Winged-men realizing that we were just two men, slowly grew bolder and began to press us. Then upon spying Prince Orton, the king's son and heir, I had an idea.

I told Tar-Gool to move with me towards the young prince.

Orton was kneeling before the throne, talking quickly to his dying father. It was evident Pondonan would be dead soon, and he was giving last minute instructions to his son—Prince Orton, who would now become the king of Caliat.

"Kill the vermin!" I could hear Pondonan gasp in a low gruff voice to his son as he coughed up blood with his dying breath. "Kill all those who oppose you! And when you become old, do not become soft like me!"

Then King Pondonan slapped his son's face with his last ounce of energy and slumped down and died. It was all most strange for me to watch. Prince Orton, showing no grief whatsoever, casually threw the body of his dead father aside like so much useless dreck, and then stood up to face me and Tar-Gool. He drew his sword and in a sudden fury recklessly charged me. This was not in vengeance or rage at my having killed his father in battle. He wanted my death because I was his enemy, an obstacle to his kingship. That kingship was something Orton had always yearned for, and now it lay within his grasp—if he would kill Tar-Gool and I before one of us killed him. He needed to stake his claim as king firmly among his people, but to do that he needed to get us out of the way. Killing us now would set him on that road to kingship in the eyes of his subjects, and more importantly, the generals and officers of the Zaran army.

Young King Orton turned out to be a very inexperience swordsmen and his foolishness in attacking me would cost him dearly. Our battle was fast and dire for the young winged brute and moments later he too lay mortally wounded at my feet. His blade had been no match for the lightning strikes of my own and he died beside the corpse of his own father. It seemed to me, somehow fitting.

Now that both kings lay dead chaos ruled and all the Zarans ran to escape our blades. Effective and orderly opposition to our attack had now evaporated and it was every Zaran for himself.

Now Tar-Gool and I made our escape, for most of the Zaran officers and courtiers who were left were concentrating on the more important matter of who should take command now. It was disgusting to watch officers and nobles fawn over the dying King Orton—who had been king of Caliat all of ten minutes—each trying to have himself named the king's successor.

Meanwhile, Tar-Gool and I made our escape out of the chamber unhindered and ran down the long hallways into another section of the huge palace. The Zaran rulers of Caliat had lost two kings that fine day and would lose many more before I would be imprisoned again at their hands. They had not yet tasted the extend of the damage I would inflict upon them.

Tar-Gool and I, though bleeding from some minor wounds, were still in good fighting shape, though my older companion suffered the worse for wear with all the strenuous swordplay he was ready, willing and able to continue the fight with me.

We soon found ourselves going down another long corridor, empty of green men and Winged-men alike. It appeared to be a part of the palace in little use. This seemed just right for our purposes.

Upon reaching the end of this corridor I saw a door slightly ajar and we opened it and ran inside the room to hide. It seemed like as good a place as any to bide our time and plan our next move. Tar-Gool planned for us to hide during the rest of that day, making a break for liberty at night when the Winged-men would be less likely to spot us from the air. It seemed like a good plan.

At the moment we found ourselves in what looked to be a large palace storage room of some kind. We discovered that it was a veritable treasure trove. Here we came upon all manner of food, weapons, jewels, furniture, silks and furs, practically anything you could think of. Much of it seemed to be personal items taken from captured of killed green people.

THE WINGED MEN | 83

"I hope we will be safe here," Tar-Gool muttered, tired, breathing hard, "It doesn't look like many of the monsters come here by the look of all this dust covering everything."

I nodded, I had noticed the dust, but I also saw footprints in that dust, so it appeared this room had more visitors than I wanted to let on to Tar-Gool at that moment. Better for my friend to rest his weary old bones and get his strength back for the trials that I knew would be ahead of us. So I kept silent and we rested and waited until dark to make our move.

What I didn't like was that the door to this storeroom had no lock on the inside. So we could only close it as tightly as we could, lay quietly, and hope that no one would enter the room and discover us. Even so, Tar-Gool and I were ready for anyone who might come calling. Our swords were out and their blades were sharp and thirsty for blood.

We took turns napping, one of us always standing guard. First me, then Tar-Gool. I slept only an hour, while Tar-Gool ate and stood guard, We sat in a small area surrounded by large crates and covered with furs and silks, as we built a small wall of crates and boxes to make our hiding place as secure as possible.

Through a small slit between the crates we could see if anyone entered the chamber, and to our surprise and alarm quite a few people did enter that room during that long day. All were young green females, obviously slaves fetching food or drink from the large pottery vessels for their Zaran masters. Thankfully, none of these slaves came to the area where we were hidden in the far back of the room, so Tar-Gool and I were relieved we did not have to deal with them. We could still keep ourselves hidden, so we felt safe for the moment.

As the day wore on Tar-Gool and I spoke often and ate and afterward I kept a sharp lookout. More green slave girls entered the room, but still none of them came near to where we were hidden. The women only stayed a few moments gathering items they had obviously been sent to collect and then were soon gone again, none the wiser about us or hiding place. It was lucky for us—and them. I was relieved that no warriors had entered the room as yet, and I was just about to compliment myself on a well-concluded plan with sundown fast approaching, when everything in our brilliant planning went to pieces. It happened like this.

With the king and his rightful heir and son dead, the Zaran officers and court of nobles had been thrown into a power-mad state of confusion and chaos. Little did Tar-Gool and I realize but at that very moment officers and petty nobles were battling it out to the death to see who would be crowned the next king of Caliat. I figured that they were probably so busy fighting each other for the power they craved that they had all forgotten about us. Perhaps even they had forgot about me, the bold fellow who had taken the lives of two of their kings in a single morning? There was no love lost between the Zarans for each other, and especially their leaders. Which was just fine with me.

As I was thinking these thoughts and watching the door from my place of concealment, I noted another beautiful woman through the dark half-light enter our rooms. She had come into the chamber quietly, then stumbled into some boxes and furniture, so that it was obvious to me she was either drunk on wine or unaccustomed to entering this room which was quite cluttered. If the latter was true, she might be a new slave, and perhaps I could find some information of value about Sirah from her. Such was my hope at the moment. As I watched her further, I noticed something familiar in the woman's walk and manner, though it was still just too dark to see her clearly.

After a time she lit an ember to better see around her in the dark room, obviously looking for something, and it was then that I was able to see her face clearly for the first time.

No wonder she looked familiar to me. It was Manalia, the mate of my best friend, and Sirah's brother, Zaor!

I looked at the woman in shock and delight. Quietly, I approached her, coming close but careful so that she did not see or hear me. I did not want to startle her or cause her to scream out in fear and alert our enemy.

The room was large, and I kept to the shadows, but soon I had reached a location behind her and was ready to make my move. In one quick motion, I grabbed Manalia in my arms, my hand locking securely over her mouth so that she could not cry out. I brought her down and quickly dragged her behind my wall of crates. All was still silence in the room and when I finally had her secure, for she fought me like a bear cub let me tell you, I quickly whispered into her ear.

THE WINGED MEN | 85

"Do not fear, Manalia. It is I, Jon Kirk! Remember me? I am a friend of your mate, Zaor, Jon Kirk."

Immediately her resistance stopped and just as quickly I let her see my face and allowed her to move freely. When she realized that I was indeed Jon Kirk, she smiled and then hugged me tightly.

"Oh, Jon Kirk, we thought you dead for sure!" she whispered joyously and in tears she could not hold back. "I never thought I would see you again. I never thought I would see another friend from the Warrior Caste again. What are you doing here?"

Quickly I told her what had befallen me since I had been abducted by the Winged-men and my meeting with Tar-Gool and our adventures since that time. I also told her of Tar-Gool and our plan to raise an army and free Caliat of the Winged-men, and of Crooch's vile treachery that had brought us here as captives before our army could march on the city. Then I told Manalia of what had transpired in the king's audience chamber and that I had killed Pondonan, the King of Caliat, as well as his son and heir. I told her that Tar-Gool and I were wanted men and in hiding now, but planning to escape at night.

Manalia just smiled at me with an enigmatic look I found curious. Then she explained. "We know all about it, Jon Kirk," she told me in a soft whisper. "Word of it has spread all through the city like the wind. The green slaves are ready to revolt, we only await the word. Meanwhile the entire city of Winged-men is out looking for you and one other, an old man. They are after your heads."

I smiled grimly, I had grown accustomed to my head being just where it was. I did not want anything to interfere with where it was presently attached.

"We are going to escape at nightfall," I said in a low voice to the girl. "Of course, you will come with us."

"Yes, thank you, Jon Kirk," Manalia replied with relief, and I saw a spark of hope now gleam in her large green eyes. "There is also one other who is a captive with me. She too must come with us."

"All right," I said carefully. "I want to be of help to you and your friend but it is only the two of us and I do not want our party to grow too large so that we will be found out or captured."

"I understand, Jon Kirk, but I think you may know this person."

I looked at Manalia curiously but said nothing. We needed to get back to Tar-Gool's fortress as soon as possible to bring the various clans and tribes under control and then lead them to the gates of Caliat before it was too late. We had a real chance now for victory with the chaos in the city and the infighting between the Zarans in their efforts to proclaim a new king. However, before I could tell this to Manalia, a noise came from the back of the room where Tar-Gool had been sleeping. The old warrior-scientist leaped from behind the crate, sword in hand, ready for battle and mayhem.

I smiled, and stayed his hand. He put down his sword and nodded. I had neglected to tell Tar-Gool that Manalia was a friend. Soon I had all explained to him in good order and the three of us were together making our plans for the future in furtive whispers.

I quickly asked Manalia what had happened after the Winged-men had attacked her village. I feared the worst for Zaor and Sirah.

"They took many of us captive," she said, remembering it all, terrified.

"What of Sirah?" I asked fearfully, barely able to restrain the question, but fearful of what I might hear in response.

Manalia sighed, then said, "That is what I was trying to tell you, Jon Kirk. Sirah is alive. She is here!"

"Alive! Here in Caliat! You have seen her?"

"Of course, she is here with me, in this very building, in a room down the hall," Manalia told me with a slight grin, seeing the great joy and relief in my face. "She was taken captive by the Winged-men also, but soon escaped from them when they stopped along the way to raid a small farm before coming here to Caliat. Sirah escaped and was making her way back home when she was spotted and captured by another band of Winged-men and then brought here as a slave."

I was surprised but delighted by this news. Sirah was alive! Sirah was here! At last, I had found my lovely Sirah! If what Manalia had just told me was true, Sirah was in a room just down the hall from me now, and what was more important, she was alive and safe. Manalia then told me that the room was less than three hundred footsteps away from this room, yet never did those hundreds of footsteps seem so far to me. At that moment it seemed to me it could be farther than all the light years between Earth and Ares.

"Is she alone?" I asked quickly. "You must bring her to me."

"No, Jon Kirk, she is not alone. There are perhaps another dozen girls and women held captive with her, and guards and many warriors they are serving. I will get a message to her to come here on some pretext, but I will not tell her why. Such joyful news would cause her to show her anxiousness and give away to the guards that something was suspicious. Let her come here unknowing that you are here, then when she sees your face it would be the best-ever surprise and joyful boon to her health in this horrible place."

I nodded, it made sense, so I told her to contact Sirah immediately.

It was beginning to get dark outside now, we had been speaking with Manalia for some time. It was getting near the hour that Tar-Gool and I had set for our escape, but now with Sirah so near, I could never leave without her. We would have to wait and Tar-Gool agreed.

Then I thought of Zaor, he had been such a good friend and a valiant warrior. I remember seeing him hit and fall in battle. I had not said anything to Manalia as yet about him, so before she set off I told her, "I am sorry…about Zaor."

Manalia looked at me curiously, "Why are you sorry for Zaor, Jon Kirk?"

"Well, I saw him fall before I was carried off by the Wingedmen," I told her softly. "I am sorry he was killed."

Manalia smiled at me with a lilting grin, "Oh, no, Jon Kirk, Zaor was not killed. He is very much alive and well. It would take much more than a blow on the head to break that hard head of his."

I smiled with great relief, happy to hear that my first friend on Ares was alive and well.

Manalia continued, "Sirah and you were carried away at the same time that King Tob fled. Zaor fully recovered from his wound and now has become the new king of the entire Warrior Caste. One day, not long ago, a group of men came to our village. They spoke with Zaor. I think one of the men, their leader, was called Sahn Jor."

So Sahn Jor had gotten through!

"Yes, he is an officer in our cause," I said, hopefully.

Tar-Gool smiled knowingly. The rumors of men massing in the mountains had been true then, the Warrior Caste lead by Zaor must be gathering together all the clans and tribes under the banner of Sahn Jor and his army. This was good news indeed!

Manalia explained, "Zaor then rode off with all the warriors to the south to aid in the attack. The attack on Caliat will come soon, Jon Kirk, your men are gathering and getting ready, the green slaves inside the city are armed and waiting word, but I do not know what day it shall all come to pass. We are all waiting. We are waiting for your word."

"Then we must escape now," I told her quickly. "Can you get Sirah and bring her here right away."

"I will try," Manalia replied, "but I must first get back to Go-pon, or he will miss me and complain. I have been here too long already. He is the overseer for my master and both a cruel and filthy beast."

As Manalia walked to the large heavy door to leave us, it suddenly burst open and a woman entered. She was the most beautiful women that I had ever seen, and my heart leapt for joy, for I saw that it was my beloved Sirah.

She was obviously surprised to see me, but instantly flew into my waiting arms. We hugged each other like we would never let go. Tears of joy streamed down her cheeks onto my own face mixing with my own tears. For that brief instant, even though we were all in such great peril, with death itself as perhaps our only escape, Sirah and I had found happiness in each other's arms. It had been a long and fearful parting but now we were one and together again.

Tar-Gool was growing impatient. After allowing us a few moments together he told us with a grim smile, "Now will you two stop that! This is not the time nor the place for love-making, Jon Kirk."

Sirah smiled, then spoke to Manalia, "I was sent by that pig Gopon to fetch you. He says you have been gone from the feast too long. He is upset and suspicious."

"The hell with him!" Manalia growled defiantly.

Sirah nodded, then turning back to me, she said, "We must do something fast, my love, for that overseer will be here soon and he may bring guards and warriors."

"Let them come!" Tar-Gool threatened, his hand grasping the hilt of his sword.

"No!" Manalia told us, "Gopon is a terrible man. A killer. If I do not get back to him he will be here soon, thinking I have escaped. He will come with many warriors."

"Then let us escape now!" I said quickly, ordering the two women to gather strips of cloth that were so abundant in the room. They quickly made a long rope out of them. I tested it and it seemed strong enough for my needs.

When the rope had been made I held it and said, "We can put this out the window and climb down it into the palace courtyard. I am sure that from there we can persuade a few kindly Zarans to help us make our escape from this city."

"Persuade?" Tar-Gool asked, smiling.

I tapped the hilt of my sword and he got the message, flashing me a grim smile.

I gave Manalia and Sirah each daggers and so armed they would be able to control their own mounts, for I planned for us to use captive Winged-men to fly us out of Caliat and to freedom. It was a good plan and we were ready to implement it.

Then the door suddenly opened and a large vicious-looking winged warrior entered the room. He was followed by a dozen more gruesome blood-thirsty winged fiends.

Manalia gasped in terror, "It is Gopon! He has come!"

Gopon and his warriors drew their swords and charged us in a headlong fury, shouting war cries of delight and death.

CHAPTER 11

CONDEMNED TO DEATH

Tar-Gool and I were ready for them and charged our attackers even before they were upon us. My blade met Gopon's and Tar-Gool was right there beside me issuing out death in wholesale lots to our enemy. Soon the fight became a wild melee of flashing swords and slashed limbs all joined by wild cries of pain and rage. Sirah and Manalia stood behind us, with their daggers drawn and ready, and they used those deadly blades on more than one occasion to aid our defense. More than once the long slim daggers used by the women drank deeply of the blood of our enemies.

We were all giving a good account of ourselves, but the end was inevitable. We were trapped and I saw that more and more reinforcements seemed to be entering the room and coming to Gopon's aid.

At this point I was being pressed hard by Gopon and two others, when suddenly I heard a terrible cry beside me and saw Tar-Gool go down. He had been cut. I could not tell how badly, but instantly Gopon left me fighting his two companions as he ran over to Tar-Gool's fallen form.

I wanted to do likewise, but I first had to dispose of these two warriors. The taller of Gopon's two men I was able to dispose of easily, quickly, and that left me with just one antagonist to dispatch. I did that soon enough, then three more guards took his place. I was pressed so hard now that I did not notice Gopon and his other men seize Manalia and Sirah until they cried out.

"Jon Kirk!" I heard Sirah shout in warning.

Instantly my heart turned to ice as I looked for her in the melee.

"Warrior!" Gopon shouted above the chaos to me. "Drop your weapon or the women die!"

In that split second I saw clearly how things stood. My heart nearly burst for I knew that I now had no choice and once again, I reluctantly threw down my sword and surrendered to my hated enemy.

I looked over and saw that Tar-Gool was down on the ground, he appeared dead from a dozen sword cuts. A cruel end to a great man, but the enemy corpses surrounding his body attested to his prowess and resolve in battle. I honored him in my mind and then went on.

Now it was just Manalia, Sirah and myself left alive, being bound and led at sword point by Gopon and his winged comrades.

Soon we were taken to the entrance of the same throne room where Tar-Gool and I had been brought before when the late and unlamented Pondonan and Orton had been kings. They were kings no more because of me.

A giant winged creature, obviously the new ruler, now sat upon the Catlianan throne. He was a larger and much more ferocious brute even than Gopon, and his largeness dwarfed many of those in the room there with him.

This new king looked down at me and smiled a grim death's head grin, showing me his long pointed teeth proudly with menace. He said, "Jon Kirk, I must thank you for doing away with the useless former king and his annoying heir, they were nothing of merit but were significant obstacles in my pathway to the throne of Caliat."

I only nodded, said boldly, "Glad I could help. Any time a Zaran king needs killing I will happily always do my best to accommodate."

While those in the chamber gasped at my bold words, and warriors drew their swords in anger, the new Zaran king merely laughed and bade them settle down. This new king, whose name I learned was Saliad, looked at me grimly and said, "As gratitude I will allow you to fight for your freedom—to fight for your miserable life as you entertain us in the Rites of Zar!"

There was a cheer from the assembled throng of Zarans, and I began to wonder just what new manner of death or doom was in store for me now with these so-called Rites of Zar.

"The women," Saliad told me mockingly, "shall become mine."

I glared at him in rage, a look that promised instant death that I would be sure to deliver to him as soon as time and circumstance allowed me to do so. But I could do nothing now. Now I was a captive at the mercy of the Zarans once again and had to bide my time.

There was great laugher among the Zaran nobles and officers when the women were taken away from me. I struggled to get free and protect them but I was held too securely.

"Filthy beast!" Manalia shouted, then spit in the direction of the king. Quickly a Zaran officer slapped her down to the ground.

When Sirah and I tried as best we could to help Manalia, we were both hit repeatedly and pulled away from her.

The Zaran nobles and officers cheered his action and our beating. Brave fellow, hitting unarmed women, I thought. I only wished I could get free and pound him as he so richly deserved, but I was held fast and secure by armed guards. The winged fiends had seen my prowess in this very chamber barely a day before so they were not taking any chances that I would be able to get free, get a sword, and then take bloody revenge upon them all.

I shouted to the Zaran king in defiant anger, "For what you have done, Saliad, you shall die! I promise you that, and also that some day soon Caliat shall fall!"

Then I was dragged away from Manalia and Sirah to some new place of imprisonment.

* * * *

The Zarans have a strange sense of humor, if you could call such a twisted mode of thought to be humor. Their laughter is rough and dark and evil. It appears that the only result of my threat to Saliad's life and the destruction of Caliat was loud and uproarious laughter. Mocking laughter. It was obvious to me that no one in that huge audience chamber ever considered the fact that I might live through the Rites of Zar to fulfill my promise to the king. No one, except me. I knew that I would survive whatever they did to me. I had to survive. I had Sirah to defend and free and I would not let her down no matter how poor my prospects looked at any particular moment. I still lived! That was my motto, the epitome of the warrior code. While there is life, there is hope, and where there is hope, there can always be victory. No one more than I knew that prospects had a knack of changing on this strange world within the blink of an eye. I endeavored to help them along as much as possible. As long as Sirah and I still lived there was hope.

Once taken outside the throne room I was separated from the women. I feared I might never see Sirah again, and I feared for her and Manalia at the hands of these vile creatures. I thought of Zaor, a good friend I'd probably never see again, and of old Tar-Gool who was already dead, his human remains now sitting at a table with his ancestors in the Afterworld for his efforts to win freedom for his people.

Gopon took the two women away, probably to the same chamber where they had been held before. They might be kept there for a while, at least for the foreseeable future. I knew that they would not be killed yet, for Zarans need all the green women they can get for breeding purposes. Only afterwards, when they have used them for their nefarious scheme, do they kill them and devour their flesh. It was a horrendous and loathsome thought, and as angry as it made me to think about it, the fact was that Zaran mating habits did at least ensure the women would be kept alive for at least a little longer. Of that I was grateful. Time was precious, every hour crucial. The women would not be killed outright, at least not immediately. That gave me some time. Some hope.

These are the dark thoughts that clouded my mind as I was led away out of the royal palace and into what looked to be some enormous civic arena in the center of the city.

I was led through this mammoth structure and then taken down to a large cell beneath that arena, then imprisoned there with many other men, all of whom were Ares green-skinned men. There were about a hundred fellow prisoners held with me, some were wounded, most half-starved, all were men from various green clans and tribes. They all stared at me in blinding fury and hate. I looked at them and wondered the reason for their reaction and animosity to me. I looked from face to face and could see that there was no one there that I knew. Not one friendly face among them. No one said a word, I could not fathom their reaction but I noticed that with menacing gestures a small group of the worst looking fellows slowly broke away from the others and came for me menacingly.

The leader of these fellows was a hulking brute of a giant, a gargantuan mountain on legs that appeared to be all bone and hard sinew. He was almost eight feet tall, the tallest green man I had ever seen, and he was dressed in the custom and manner of the fierce Ag Nomads. They were known throughout the planet for their terrible ferocity and fighting ability.

As he came closer, one of his companions made a lunge for me on my flank, but before I could be touched, the giant caught him and lifted the man over his head and threw him twenty feet against the far wall of the cell. I was astonished at the strength of the fellow and the fact that he had apparently come to my aid. Or had he? Everyone there laughed, but they soon quieted down when the giant commanded them to be silent with a gruff bark. The men shut up instantly. I stood there defiant, waiting, ready for his attack and to defend myself accordingly. It was evident that every prisoner in that cell feared this man, maybe even more than they feared the Winged-men themselves. Perhaps they were right to be so careful of this giant and his rage. I certainly had no desire to do battle with him but sometimes the battle comes to me and there is little I can do to stop it. So be it!

"I am Darg. Here, I am king," the giant barked at me. Then arrogantly he ordered me, "You will bow down to Darg and kiss my feet. Prove to me that you are worthy of Darg allowing you to live one more miserable day."

I just looked at him and laughed. "Are you serious?"

Darg just laughed back at me and others there followed his lead, though there were many more I noticed in the background who did not laugh. They were eager to see a fight and this looked to them like it might be a good one.

"Little man, you will be crushed by Darg!" the giant barked at me.

I smiled, "Well, Darg, I am sorry, but I can not allow you to do that."

"Hah!" he barked, beating his chest in anger. "You will bow down to me or be crushed1"

"I do not think that I will bow down to any dirty, filthy, *chavas*!" I told him boldly. It had been a defiant move and perhaps my sentence of death at his hands. In the Ares language, the *chavas* is a particularly large and repulsive rat-like creature that exists on waste and decayed matter. So what I had called Darg meant some pretty strong and nasty insulting stuff in Ares terms. Of course my words had the desired effect upon him. They got Darg mad. Very, very mad.

Darg did not appreciate my insult and turned livid with rage. Others in the jail cell smiled with anticipation, cheering the giant on, telling him to break me into tiny pieces. I looked over at Darg and swallowed hard, for I could see that he was entirely capable to doing just that, or worse if I allowed him. My play was not to allow him to do anything to me. Others in the cell looked on fearfully, knowing too well from previous bouts what would be in store for me and I could see their feelings were on my side. As short lived as my life might appear to them.

"Loathsome worm! Cowardly dog!" Darg barked an enraged command at me one last time. "Bow down to your master!"

I found it interesting that he was giving me one more chance to surrender. I nodded, letting him see a bit of fear enter my features, and I answered softly, "Perhaps you are right, Darg. You are the master here."

He looked at me sharply, smiling broadly in victory.

I allowed a wry grin and bowed slightly, always keeping my eyes on him at all moments, and then I rose to quickly give him a huge blockbuster punch deep into his rather formidable stomach. Darg howled and immediately doubled over gasping for breath.

"All hail, Darg," I proclaimed with a grim laugh. "Master of the *Chavas*!"

At that insult the entire cell full of men laughed brutally. Darg, seeing a man near him laughing with the rest, garbed the fellow and bashed his head against the stone wall with a resounding plop. I saw the man's skull crack like an eggshell.

"More food for the winged vermin!" Darg said loudly, and now all the laughing had stopped dead.

I maneuvered myself around the cell trying to get into a good position for what I knew was on the way.

"Come here, stranger," Darg told me, feigning friendship. "I like you. You have spunk. Come here and fight Darg."

I shrugged. It was inevitable after all. This is what I had wanted and waited for. This battle had to be, for there could never be two leaders in these cells and among the prisoners. I was not going to allow anyone to stop me from doing what I had to do to escape from here and to save Sirah.

However, Darg would be no easy man to take down. He was extremely powerful and much larger than I was, but because of the lesser gravity of the planet Ares as opposed to that of my home world of Earth, I was actually just as strong and powerful as he was. Perhaps even stronger? However, no one knew that yet. I was sure that Darg was in for quite a shock when the battle began. He just didn't know my powers, but he would discover them soon enough. My Earthly strength was a fact that I would gladly turn to my advantage and I began to set up Darg for a heavy unsuspecting fall.

I smiled, told Darg, "This shall make for an interesting match."

Darg barked enraged insults and then charged me headlong like a crazy man who was going to tear me apart piece by piece with his bare hands. I had no doubt that such would have been the result on my end, had I not had my Earthly muscles to give me the added speed and strength where I more than met the match of his attack. He was utterly shocked by my defense to his most brutal blows. I gave him back shot for shot as good as he gave me, pounding him unmercilessly, heavily. He was more surprised, then a bit fearful. The fight went on for a long time, a pounding battle of vicious, no-holds-barred mayhem. After the usual hard slugs and breadbasket punches, each of us seemed to be giving as good as we got. It was not long before such an intense battle was wearing us both down. We were tiring. Nearing exhaustion. As yet neither of us had achieved a knock-out punch or a death blow.

At first, after Darg's initial attack and repulse, I had the advantage. Darg simply could not believe my strength and it kept getting him in trouble when he did not take that into consideration in his actions. He paid a terrible price and was hurt badly, but the fellow was stout and a tough fighter. After a while Darg finally realized the truth of my prowess—he was not the sharpest antagonist I had ever fought—but after taking many surprise shots he became much more wary and fought me smarter. He did not come at me so foolishly with headlong attacks. He also grew more serious. He was hurt and tired and now he was not sure if he was going to win this fight or not. That fact scared Darg. It was a feeling the giant had never encountered in battle before. He'd never lost a fight in his life. He did not believe it was even possible, until now, but it was happening right now before his eyes. It shattered his confidence, but it made him a better and more dangerous antagonist than ever he was before.

Darg was taking some incredible pounding, but he kept coming back and he was giving me a good drubbing as well. Blood was spraying all around the cell, all over us, and on many of the men there imprisoned in that cell who scrambled to get out of our way. Even as their frantic eyes could not look away from our monumental battle, and they ran their tongues over their lips anticipating one of our deaths very soon.

Darg's blows landed on me like hammers and my head was ringing, though all I could hear by then was the sound of the crowd, their roars and cheers. They had began shouting encouragement to Darg, but now they were cheering for me. My fellow prisoners were openly cheering me on. It was good to hear. I wondered how long it would last and how long I would last.

Some of Darg's friends did not like this show of support for me and struck out against those cheering me on, so that soon a dozen smaller brawls had broken out to accompany our main event of the evening. All was soon utter chaos as a result.

The fights around me raged on for a while, then there were screams and fearful yells, and men began to die. It was Darg's few friends among the group, just four or five hard-headed comrades, who were now being set upon by the other prisoners they had abused for so long.

Now a couple of men who obviously had something against Darg boldly jumped the giant from behind and started to beat him. He just stopped the fight with me then, putting our bout on hold with an arm gesture, then casually picked up both men over his head, and effortlessly threw them into the crowd around us with a loud defiant roar. I was grateful for the brief respite.

Darg's attack was an amazing feat of strength that I could not help but respect.

With a great laugh, Darg gave me a sinister smile, then he charged me once again.

I sighed, stood ready; this guy was proving one tough cookie.

"You are truly the equal of the mighty Darg," Darg told me in gasps, and for the first time I heard respect enter his mighty voice. "What are you called? What is your name?"

For answer I gave Darg another uppercut deep into his massive stomach. He bowed back stunned. Everyone in the cell laughed at that and his reaction. Even Darg himself. They all seemed to find that sort of battle humor very funny here on Ares.

"My name is Jon Kirk," I said, laughing myself now, "Remember that name!"

"I shall remember it, Jon Kirk," Darg growled.

However, now Darg did not laugh, but with deadly business he crossed with a sudden right that connected squarely on my chin and I went flying backwards a good ten feet, back to the bars of the cell, then down to the floor flat on my ass. I was stunned.

Darg walked towards me slowly, then said, "Jon Kirk, your chin presents a most unguarded target that I could not resist."

"Obviously," I replied nursing my sore jaw. It wasn't broken, but it sure felt like it was. That fellow hit hard.

Darg stopped then and laughed at my sorry plight. He immediately gained back his confidence and that would be his undoing.

I looked up at the giant, towering over me. He moved back from me and I stood up, which I was surprised that he allowed me to do. I gave him a grim smile, then I charged him, my head hitting him square and hard in the breadbasket once more, and this time mighty Darg went down, and this time he blacked out unconscious.

Well, that was hopefully the end of it. Everyone in our jail cell had certainly enjoyed the show and they all congratulated me on a job well done. Then as if remembering old scores, some of the prisoners jumped upon the prone form of Darg using anything they could to vent their anger and hatred upon him.

I could not allow this and did what I could to stop it.

"What honor is this?" I shouted, quickly pulling the men off Darg. "Leave him be. He fought well. He fought with honor."

The last man I dragged off Darg was obviously twisted by his hatred for the giant, or perhaps even insane, for he giggled and gibbered relentlessly like some lunatic. He shouted , "Now, Darg shall feed the Winged-men!"

Then the madman ran away and hid in a corner by himself, jabbering in whispers to unseen friends or foes. Ghosts only his addled mind could see. It was all quite disconcerting to witness but such was the effect on some men held in such vile captivity over long periods of time with nothing but death staring them in the face.

Upon closer inspection of Darg's body I noticed that some coward had slipped a dagger into his heart. Even worse, I saw that one of his massive hands had been cut off and was not with the corpse. It had been taken away from the body as some kind of prize. I soon found the missing hand hidden in the tunic of the madman.

"That is Orlaz the madman," a young warrior named Tazo told me. "Both of his brothers were killed by Darg in a fight. It was in a fair fight, but Orlaz was a coward and he did not come to his brother's aid when summoned by them. They called out to him to help them but he held back, he refused the call of his own blood. His mind snapped because of the guilt of his dishonorable action."

"I see," I replied. "He is a poor creature."

"Are not we all?" Tazo continued with a sharp look at me. "Pawns to be used in these Rites of Zar, or whatever they may be."

I nodded and further asked Tazo, and his brother, Dameton, to explain to me about the Rites of Zar.

"Different games make up the Rites of Zar for different days of the games," Dameton explained. "The first one is called the Games of The Zarans. These are not so popular with the Zaran hosts because they force Zarans to fight against each other. The second day of the games are the Games of Ares, in which hundreds of green men are given swords to fight to the death against each other in the arena for the amusement of our Zaran masters. The Zarans enjoy this day of the games very much."

"I can believe that they do," I said grimly.

"And yet," Tazo now continued, taking over the explanation from his brother, "the third day is the game they love the best. For that day is known as The Graduating Exercise. In this game, and I use the word advisedly, a force of unarmed green men has to fight against a force twice their number of armed and trained Zaran Winged-men. It is no real fight at all. It is slaughter, pure and simple."

I sighed, it was as I expected from such brutal and cruel creatures.

I asked Tazo, "Why don't they just kill us off and get it over with?"

"That would be too easy, Jon Kirk. Don't you see?" Tazo told me with a grim smile, "that would not allow any amusement for the Zarans. They enjoy these great bloody spectacles of blood and death."

I nodded, I should have known better with what I had seen of the Zarans since I had come to Ares but I still held some hope for them, for their humanity? But I had been proved wrong over and over again. Apparently they had no humanity or mercy whatsoever, and that meant they had to be dealt with eventually, but not as honored enemies, but as vermin and pests that must be eradicated. Old Tar-Gool was apparently correct in his opinion of the Zarans.

"How long do we have before they call for us?" I asked, fearing the answer, thinking of my beloved Sirah. Would I ever see her again?

"In three days time, the Rites of Zar begin," Tazo told me with a hopeless sigh. "Our game shall be on the third and last day of the Rites. It is five days hence to our appointment with death, Jon Kirk."

Here was a gloomy fellow, I thought, and yet, he was one who had plenty of reason for that gloom. Nevertheless, I did my best to stem the tide of defeatism. I spoke to each prisoner, found out information about each one, and it came to pass that as I did so, I soon realized that my defeating Darg in single battle and my optimism made me the new de facto leader of these wretched fellows. So I took on my new role of leader of the prisoners, or as I called myself, commander. I told all of them that I reasoned that since we were all going to die, then we should make it our duty to do all we could to take as many Zarans along with us into the pit of death as we could. I convinced them that it was far better than just standing around feeling sorry for ourselves and waiting to be hacked into a dozen pieces by our enemies.

As a fighting man, it made sense to me to have such an outlook. I would sell my life dearly. Others also joined me in my thoughts on the matter and the battle ahead.

No sooner had I finished explaining this new fact of defiance to my fellow prisoners than Tazo and I began making plans. We gathered prisoners and spoke to them of plans for our eventual escape. Tazo and Dameton brought over another prisoner named Andu who joined us. The four of us talked over our options. We still had five days, and in five days we could whip these men into some kind of disciplined and skilled fighting force. With any luck we could give the Zarans some games they would never forget.

Andu, who was a warrior by trade, actually knew Zaor and Soak, and with his three Sar Nomad companions, were all excellent swordsmen. They formed the nucleus of my fighting force.

The next morning we began our training schedule, every man in that cell pledged his life and honor to our venture to fight for our escape. Or if not, then to give the Winged-men a battle they would not soon forget and to kill as many of the enemy as possible.

From that morning on; Tazo, Dameton, Andu and the three Sar Nomads who were with him, taught the other prisoners all they knew about the fighting arts and how to use a sword in battle. Their talent was considerable. With the few sticks we were able to smuggle into the cell, we began teaching swordsmanship to as many men as possible. Many of these captives had not held a sword in a long time. And while I was convinced that we would eventually all die in battle in the arena—of this I was afraid there could be no doubt—where before these men shivered in terror of certain death, now they looked death straight in the face with cold defiance.

Now these men had a cause that bound them together as brothers, something important to fight for—even if it was just to kill as many Zarans as we could. For most men that was enough. So we kept busy, I kept them busy. Now they had a goal to work for, training and exercises on offensive fighting in all ways, but especially by hand in teams against the enemy, with the aim of getting their swords. Then we trained them in effective swordplay. As the days passed I noted most of the men improving on their fighting skills considerably. Under my guidance, and with my companions, these men now had been molded into an adequate fighting force that made me proud.

Soon we were ready for the games, even looking forward to them.

CHAPTER 12

THE RITES OF ZAR

Finally the day of reckoning was upon us, the third day of the Rites of Zar had arrived. Now my group of 135 unarmed green men were ready to go up against twice that number of fully armed Zaran warriors. Terrifying flying monsters.

These were the dread Games of Commencement, or the Graduating Exercise, wherein young Zaran warriors entering adulthood participated in bloody ritual slaughter for the first time in their lives. It would presage their actions for the rest of their lives. The premise behind it all was that they were supposed to prove what mighty and fierce warriors they were—what great killers they were. They were to prove this by cutting down as many unarmed defenseless green men as possible. It was mindless slaughter and a disgrace to true honor of any fighting man.

"The corpses of both groups of the dead—for invariably some few Winged-men are often killed as well as the hundreds of green men—are afterwards fed to the Zarian people. It is what many of the poor Zarans live upon," said a young warrior named Coron. He had been placed with us because he had killed two Winged-men when he had begun a failed revolt in the streets of Caliat. He was a good man who had fought bravely for his ideals and had been placed in here to die with us in the arena.

Not all of the men in the cell with us knew about this further evidence of the grisly nature of the evil Winged-men and their so-called customs and society. Such information only made each of us that much more determined to fight harder and to somehow win our freedom.

In those five days of hard training my men made notable progress. They were now a well-trained and disciplined fighting force, eager to do battle with the enemy. I divided them into two groups.

The first group contained those I considered the best swordsmen that we had. The best fighters. The second group was of men of lesser ability, older, younger, less fit, but still full of the fire in their belly for a fight. This second group was headed by Coron, who I considered my best commander. My plan was simple, and we all went over it quickly one last time as we were marched in chains upstairs to await our entrance into the arena.

The arena in Caliat was about the size of a football field back on Earth. In the stands it seemed the entire Zaran population of the city was in attendance cheering their warriors. I could see their new king, Saliad, in his royal booth surrounded by officers and nobles. In the front of that booth, I spied Gopon holding the leashes of two chained green female slaves. One was Manalia, and the other was my beloved Sirah. My heart pounded fearfully for them.

Then loud horns were blown signaling it was time for the games to begin.

In single file we were marched into the flat dirt surface of the area and formed a line lengthwise. Across the field from us were two opposing lines of winged Zarans, double our number of trained and armed creatures thirsting for our blood. They were ready to kill. Ready to be set loose upon us. We were apparently ready to be slaughtered. It was that simple. But it would not be so, if I had anything to do about it.

We were unchained. Instead of running or falling down in crying tears as in previous such events, my men stood their ground tall and proud, stoic, ready for the fight that was to come. Each man knew what he had to do. Each man stood by ready for action. We waited for the Zaran attack to begin. Andu, who was on my right, and Tazo, on my left, suddenly were feigning a heated argument. They mocked each other jokingly.

"I tell you, Tazo," Andu said boldly, "there are at least 250 of them."

"No, my friend, there are 270," Tazo had counted.

"I counted 250," Andu repeated earnestly. "Why, your eyes can not even see them properly."

"My eyes are fine and I can count far better than you can." Tazo said with a laugh.

"Shut up, both of you!" I ordered with a laugh. "We'll have plenty of time for this argument after the battle. They'll be here soon enough, then you can count them one by one as you kill them."

Tazo and Andu nodded and smiled, they liked that conclusion.

A drum was beaten and then some kind of trumpet was blown in shrill warning. Now King Saliad stood up to the cheering of the crowd of Zaran people, and with a wave of his sword and another accompanying cheer of the bloodthirsty throng, the Rites of Zar began.

I looked over at Andu and Tazo and gave them a slight grin, "By the way you two, you are both wrong. There are only 260 of them."

We all laughed, restless, nervous laughter.

Tazo smiled said, "Well, that's better already, Jon Kirk, for now there are ten less of them than I thought."

I nodded, then ordered loudly, "Okay, everyone get set, you know your positions. They are getting ready to charge us. You all know what you have to do."

My orders were passed down our long line of men. They were ready, eager for battle, for revenge.

Then as one in perfect unison, the Zaran Winged-men drew their swords and slowly and contemptuously walked swiftly towards us with slaughter in their cold cruel eyes. There would be no quarter given today in this fight, that was for sure. None asked either.

There was a sudden silence from the crowd now, as everyone watched, their eyes transfixed on the two ranks of advancing Zaran warriors.

Behind us I heard talk from the spectators, as wagers were hurriedly being placed, harsh cries for blood and murder were sounded, and threats were made against us in our last few moments of life.

"Something is wrong here," I heard one Zaran spectator say to another in obvious concern. "These green cattle do not run away or cry for mercy like all the others have done in the past games."

"Why, that is only because they are so petrified with fear, Yarno. You know, I have two winglets at the other end of the field today. They each promise to bring me back as many greenling heads as they can carry."

I ignored the words from those in the stands and concentrated on the enemy as they advanced upon us. Then I gave the order.

Quickly, and as one man, we split into our two groups. I took command of the group of better swordsmen as planned, even though we had no swords as yet. I had Andu, Tazo and Dameton as my lieutenants. We had no swords given to us by our captors, so we would take our weapons from our enemy.

Behind us now, lead by Coron, came our less proficient fighters, shielded and in a place of temporary safety for the moment. My plan was to have our best fighters up front, where they would kill as many Zarans as possible—and take as many swords as they could from the enemy to arm our own men. Once armed, my better swordsmen would cut a bloody swath through the surprised enemy. At least, so was my plan.

"Take their swords, then give them to our unarmed fighters." I ordered my men. It was a dangerous game we were playing, but it was the only hope we had. We needed to get swords to defend ourselves and there was only one place to get them. From the enemy. "Kill the Zarans and take their weapons! Then arm our men so we can fight and kill more of the enemy!"

My men cheered these words and they all knew what they had to do.

I quickly ordered my men to form into a large V formation, like the flying wedge that had been banned in American football so long ago. That formation would prove useful now. The advancing Zarans and many of the spectators watched us curiously, no doubt wondering what we were doing, but the enemy continued their march towards us and we could see they were wondering just what we were doing as well.

Then I gave the order and we boldly charged!

Cries of shock and surprise and eventually laughter rang from the audience at our unexpected and bold action, yet once they realized what was happening, the spectators began to shout for their warriors to attack us. By then it was just too late for them. The audience was shocked, perhaps even scared by what they were seeing. I knew that we would give them a show they would never forget. The Zaran warriors did not seem scared, but they were surprised, trying to figure out just what we were up to. That was good.

That would be their undoing. They were very confident. They had no fear of "green cattle" as they called us.

At a wild run we charged the thin double line of Zaran Winged-men that stretched across the arena. I lead my men straight on into the enemy, we hit them so quick and hard that fully a dozen Zarans lay dead upon the blood-soaked ground of the arena in our first attack. Immediately we took their swords and daggers from their corpses, and any other weapons they had, then quickly distributed them to our unarmed men. Those men now were armed and fought only harder and caused more damage to the shocked enemy, who had expected a simple and easy slaughter. More Zarans fell dead, still more of my men too up their weapons to use them against our winged enemy. The slaughter was turning against them now.

Having some of my men armed with swords meant that we had a real chance in this fight, if not to win, at least to make the Zarans pay a steep blood price for their victory. We would make sure that it proved to be a bittersweet victory for them, if victory it was to be.

I smiled as I saw four more Winged-men go down to vicious sword blows from my men. I myself took one Zaran in the neck, hitting and slashing him with all my power, almost severing his ghastly head from his shoulders. My attack was forcing his comrades to move off. It showed their cowardice by them moving away from me and going after an easier target—one of my unarmed men. I was not going to allow that man to fall to our enemy. I was by his side in a flash, defending him, plunging my sword through a Zaran throat for his vileness. Then I took my fallen enemy's sword and gave it to the formerly unarmed green man. That man thanked me quickly and promptly used his new sword to stick a nearby winged brute and kill the creature dead.

By now the Zaran line was in utter confusion. We had split their force into two parts, so that now their two groups were cut off from each other. Now many of their troops away from us were rendered ineffective in the fight and out of action. I knew this would only be a temporary situation, so in the meantime I had my men do as much damage as possible to the ranks of their primary force. We did.

After that initial surprise attack by my forces, and the traumatic shock that had resulted in the enemy ranks, we saw the end of any organized Zaran fighting. Now, it was every man for himself on the enemy side, even as our own men grew bolder, gained still more weapons, armed ourselves to a man, and then moved forward with our plan of coordinated attack. We were a much stronger force of fighters now and that meant that the Winged-men, while more numerous, had grown much weaker by our battle. We took advantage of that fact in renewing our attack, this time with most of my men armed.

It got so bad for our enemy that many of the Zarans had to take to the air, seeking to escape our sword blows by flying over our heads where we could not get at them. They flapped around on their huge dark wings, trying to lop off the heads of my men who were still unarmed. They succeeded in some cases, the cowards! My armed men did all they could to protect those who were unarmed, but it was difficult and some unarmed men were killed.

Since not all my men were yet armed, some of them succumbed to this new tactic of slaughter, even as they tried to fight off the winged creatures and massed in groups for mutual protection. However, we were able to bring down some of the flying creatures using ropes, and once my men got an enemy warrior on the ground, we made sure that he never flew again.

By now all was chaos in the arena and my remaining men were scattered all over the field as were the Zarans. They flew around the battlefield dealing out death from above whenever they saw an opportunity and where they could do so safely. The cowards would only go after my men who were unarmed. Those men who were armed were doing a good job of taking down the flying creatures and dealing death to them as well. It was turning into a bloody slaughter on both sides now. The Zaran crowd raged in horror, aghast and unbelieving at what was happening before their own eyes, but I think their innate cruel inner hearts loved the bloody spectacle nevertheless.

The brief optimism I had felt earlier from our initial surprise attack had evaporated now in the harsh reality of this wild battle. With overwhelming numbers of winged fighters against us everywhere, and with their ability to fly, the Zarans were hurting us badly because now they were coming down upon my men in groups and from the rear. It was a new strategy that was working for them.

It was beginning to look very grim for my side, and it was not long before there were only about fifty of my fighters still alive. I gathered them all together in one group. I noticed that almost all the lesser swordsmen who had formed up in Coron's group had been killed. The only consolation to this terrible tragedy was that I knew now that all those who remained alive were because of my bold plan. These then were my best swordsmen and fighters. Every one of them was loaded with captured enemy weapons and ready to fight to the death!

I saw that Tazo had fallen early in the battle, and afterwards his brother, Dameton, had been caught and run down in a trap. I had seen him carried high into the air by two Winged-men who then released him to plummet hundreds of feet to his death. It was a terrible scene to witness and to be helpless to stop. It was also a big blow to our side to lose two such fine warriors and friends.

I gathered my remaining fighters together into a corner of the arena. Here we stood defiantly with sword points facing the enemy and our backs to the wall. There was no where else to go now. At least we were protected from an attack on our rear while we concentrated on the Zarans coming at us on foot and from the air. For some time we were able to hold our ground. We knew the Zarans had to come to us, and we could see that they were becoming increasingly reluctant to do so.

The crowd was mad with blood lust and excitement, chanting for their side, and urging them onward to attack us and kill us all. The spectators initially had been totally supportive of their winged fellows, but as the battle raged and the bodies piled up, they began to have second thoughts. While none of them offered us any support, some grudgingly admitted the green slaves had given an exceptional account of themselves this day. That is what I wanted to achieve. Now I wanted to go even further!

Suddenly I noticed something strange that I could not figure out. One minute I looked up and it was there, the next time I looked up, it was not there. What had I just seen? I could scarcely understand it. By that time we were so deeply involved in the battle and the killing lust was upon us all that none of us would have noticed much else, other than an earthquake at that point. What soldiers call the fog of war had us all within its grasp, green men and Winged-men alike, solidly within its power. The audience was

THE WINGED MEN | 109

all eyes upon us as they watched in frantic attention, a screaming mass delighting in the death throes of our too-quickly diminishing band of fighters—what they all thought were merely arrogant green cattle that had fought back like trained warriors.

However, as I looked up as a winged creature flew by my head, I noticed the strange apparition once again that had caught my attention earlier. I saw it better this time and could barely believe what I had seen. It looked like some kind of huge covering of some kind, actually more like a monstrous net. I was astonished. I realized that it was an exact copy of a much larger net that I knew had been designed by the master scientist, Tar-Gool.

Tar-Gool was a man who had the means and the power to accomplish almost anything on the planet Ares, and one of his inventions had been the creation of a huge metal net that could be placed over the entire city of Caliat. It had been an ambitious project and a brilliant idea, if it worked. He had created the plan to use this net to subdue the flight of the Zarans, but it had not been erected. But I saw now that something much like it had been built, but on a much smaller scale made to fit over the arena. It was being put in place as I watched. It looked like it was working too, now being set in place above our heads. I stared at it in disbelief.

I was to learn later that Zaor and Sahn Jor had modified Tar-Gool's plan somewhat into something a lot more practical. Since almost the entire Zaran population of Caliat was in the arena this day, Zaor had wisely decided to build and deploy a much smaller version of Tar-Gool's net. This took much less time and energy to constrict and was faster to deploy than the idea of a massive city-wide net. Zaor moved to have his net placed over the arena before he and his army made their attack on the city. It was a bold move.

Many Zarans, of course, had noticed the net as it had been put up over the arena. Most of them had merely wondered what it might be, perhaps some new part of the games? By then they were all so involved in the games and the blood lust that they did not notice or care about much other than the killing they saw before them. Zaran over confidence was such that few could ever conceive of the fact that this could be some kind of attack on their city. Their society had such customs that it never occurred to them that in time of trouble they should warn their fellows. How this huge net was put up over the top of the arena by Zaor and his men

I did not know, but it was a welcome sight let me tell you. Now the Winged-men were all trapped in the arena, but they did not quite realize it yet.

As for me and my men, by that time we were in dire trouble fighting off the winged enemy and I hoped that whatever was going on above with the net and Zaor's men, that his attack would begin soon so that he could come to our aid.

As the precious minutes ticked away my men took sword cut and wounds, many of them fatal. By now my group of fighters was down to only twenty left standing, but we were still holding off a relentless attack from the Zarans. They smelled blood now and victory, so they came at us harder. My men and I were getting quite nervous by that time, things did not look good for us. We had all seen the huge net descend over the arena and we knew what that meant. So did the Zarans by this time, some trying to take flight and escape, but they discovered that it was impossible. The net held firm and kept them locked within the arena better than any prison cell.

My men cheered and we fought only the harder. The Zaran line wavered, then fell back in chaos.

We watched as other Winged-men tried to escape by going underground, or using the ground level exits, but there were large bottlenecks at every one of these exits now as well. For you see, we soon learned that the green slaves within the city had revolted against their masters and were now causing havoc among the Zaran defenders. At the same time an army of green warriors from all corners of Ares led by Zaor had the city under siege and had fully breached the walls.

So it turned out to be that the attack on Caliat had become a neat package all wrapped up just as we had intended—though not happening exactly as we had planned. None of the Zarans in the arena were able to escape the city through the gates, and none were able to fly away because of the net covering the arena. They were quite nicely trapped. Trapped like rats and scurrying all over in any attempt to flee.

By this time there was a renewed Zaran force of perhaps one hundred warriors pressing us and there were even some members of the audience who drew their own swords and joined in the attack upon us as well. These were quickly dispatched by my men as the battle raged. But we took our losses as well.

It was not long before only Coron, Andu, myself and six others were left standing with swords flashing defiantly. We cut deeply into our enemy, bringing down Zaran after Zaran, the dirt of the arena now soaked with their blood. We were now only nine left of the original 135 green men who had entered the arena with me to be slaughtered in the Games. Now I saw the cause of the massive bottleneck at one of the exits to the arena. I saw that it was Zoar's warriors mounted on large, fierce reptilian *pourks* streaming through the exit and charging into the arena. Their swords were drawn and in bloodthirsty rage they were taking a heavy toll of any Zarans that were in their way. They cut them down by the dozens, a bloody harvest.

Meanwhile, at another gate, I saw Ogz and Armen, two men who had once been deadly enemies, ride side by side as friends now, as they happily attacked and killed Winged-men. They had hundreds of mounted men riding behind them as they battled as brothers against the Winged-men trapped in that section of the arena.

Through a third gate I now saw Sahn Jor and his troops enter the arena. These men had originally been only woodworkers, but today they were not armed with hammers and saw, but with swords and pikes. Better yet, they had bows and arrows and were using them to deadly effect to shoot the trapped Winged-men out of the sky. Now there really was no escape for any Zaran. The arrows were doing a tremendous job of thinning the numbers of the Winged-men still left alive, and it was really causing utter panic in their ranks now.

I noticed that through another exit came another group of wild green men. It was Tavan with his Southern Farmers pushing through the press of winged defenders, mowing them down efficiently and quickly, and then breaking through as they sent any remaining enemy fighters quickly into the Afterworld.

With time to spare, Tavan and his force worked their way through the crowds and were able to get to my small group and save us from further attack, for my men were all done in. Tavan's men broke through the last remaining Zaran defenders, and brought us out safely from behind the pile of Zaran corpses we had used as a shield and defensive perimeter.

By that time there were only five of us left alive: Coron, Andu, two of the huge Sar Nomads—Iko and Tumat—and myself. Five men had survived out of my original group of 135 men. It was a sobering realization. We were able to stop our fighting now and look around us at the devastation going on with such frenzy. We watched in awe as the slaughter of the Winged-men of Caliat turned into the extinction of the Zarans of Caliat. For it was that simple. Revenge ran rampant and deep and the green men of Ares had the blood frenzy of revenge upon them. They had much to pay the Zarans back for. I could not blame them at all after what I had heard the Zarans had done to the green people of this world for thousands of years. With my own eyes I had seen such horrors as convinced me that not one Zaran winged monster should be left alive.

The Zarans of Caliat were trapped now, desperate but unable to escape. Not one winged monster in that huge arena could escape the net that kept them all prisoners. They were forced to fight, but it was a fight they could never win now. All they could do now was fight and die. And they were dying all around us as green men and women everywhere cut them down and cheered in victory and freedom.

Armen, Zaor, and Sahn Jor rode up to me in a triumphant canter.

"Jon Kirk, you still live!" Zaor shouted in joy.

"Yes, and one might say the same for you, Zaor!" I shouted back happily. I had seen my friend struck down in battle by Tob's henchmen and feared he was dead.

"Jon Kirk!" they shouted as they rode over. "Jon Kirk!"

I smiled at these three friends, then asked Sahn Jor, "Is the city taken?"

"Yes, my lord," he replied, saluting me.

I acknowledged his salute and returned it with one of my own. I was surprised by him using a title when addressing me, but said nothing of it for now, as there were far more pressing things to consider than mere titles.

"We thought you lost and dead, Jon Kirk," Zaor told me with a grin. "And that old rascal, Tar-Gool, too. By the way, where is he hiding?"

"He was killed by the Zarans," I said with some sadness at the thought of his death. By the look upon the faces of the men around me I saw that each of them felt the bitter loss of old Tar-Gool. He was a man who turned out to be not what he first seemed to be at all, but he was a patriotic fellow in his own way and even turned out to be a good friend.

The city of Caliat would not be free if Tar-Gool had not begun his plan that brought everyone together on this mission. We grieved for Tar-Gool and soon his name was taken up by our fighting men as a war cry as we continued to mercilessly mow down the remaining Zaran defenders and cleared them from Caliat.

"Remember Tar-Gool!" the warriors shouted. "Remember Tar-Gool!"

"Zaor," I asked, "come with me. Sirah and Manalia are here in the city and we must find them."

"Manalia?" I thought I had left her safe back at home," he replied shocked and angry now. "How did she get here? Where is she?"

"It's a long story, my friend," I told him, but I explained some of what she had told me as Zaor and I rode over to the large grandstand where Saliad, the last Zaran king of Caliat, reposed in amazement in his private box surrounded by a dozen of his personal bodyguard. The ones that still remained loyal. I looked over and chanced to see the wily Gopon with Manalia and Sirah in another unguarded box over to the side. Zaor and I headed straight for him at a frantic run with swords out.

We soon reached the end of the unguarded box and upon seeing us advance upon him, Gopon, who proved to us he was as ardent a coward as one could be, immediately fled, leaving the women behind. We let him go. Now Sirah and I were together again and in each other's arms. I smiled as we saw Zaor and Manalia embracing as well.

By that time we were safely out of the battle and I just wanted to stay with my beloved Sirah and protect her from further harm. It had been a long and hard struggle and an emotional reunion.

As we watched, we saw that methodically the remaining Zarans in the city of Caliat were being effectively mowed down until the last of them, trying desperately to escape our swords and full of panic now, took flight up to the height of the net. There they were still not safe, for Tavan's skilled archers shot them down with their arrows by the dozens. The results were devastating upon the remaining defenders. Now outright panic seized the enemy ranks. The battle turned to slaughter, but it was nothing less than they had given, and nothing more than they deserved.

Soon the battle fizzled and turned into a mopping up operation, and the only spot of resistance was the Royal Box where King Saliad and his few remaining retainers were vainly trying to hold out against the inevitable. They would not surrender and we did not really want them to do so.

I now led troops with Sahn Jor, and Zaor by my side in an attack that would be spoken of in poems and sung in songs by the green people of Ares for many years. Poems and songs would be sung about how on that hot afternoon in Caliat Jon Kirk had slain his third Zaran king. Of how, by my sword, King Saliad now lay dead. Soon all the Zarans in the city of Caliat joined him in death. The few that remained were hunted down and exterminated by teams of green warriors. The city was soon free and the Zarans were all dead, a terrible memory and no more.

Cheers went up all around me and rang throughout the city from every quarter by the freed green men and women who had been kept as slaves and were now free.

"This is a great victory and a joyous time for every man and woman on our world," Sahn Jor said full of happiness, but his eyes showed he thoughtfully remembered the price that had been paid to achieve it. It had been a high price in blood and death. "But we can not rest now. We must remember that there are five more Zaran cities that must be taken, and they must be sacked and their slaves freed before their warriors have a chance to attack us, or retake this city. Very soon now they shall hear the news of the fall of Caliat and they will be forewarned by our actions here. These other cities will not be as easy to bring down now."

"They will be ready for us," Zaor added. "We will be ready for them, too."

I nodded, "I am sure that even now they are preparing to move against us," I told my lieutenants. "There is no time to lose, we must gather our forces, arm everyone, and fortify this city before we bring the war to the enemy."

* * * *

Later, I walked alone with Sirah along the parapets of the wall around Caliat. We talked of many things as we surveyed the damage to the city and the great losses to our side. We spoke of our love for each other and our joy that we were finally together again. We had lost many friends and fine warriors in this battle. It had been a bloody victory, but it was worth it.

"We paid dearly for this victory, my love," I told Sirah.

She gave me a wan smile, then wrapped her arms around me and brought her luscious green lips up to my own. She kissed me softly and whispered, "We are together, Jon Kirk. I am happy. I knew you would save me. I knew we would be free and together. And now Caliat is free and the Winged-men are no more. That is not such a high price, my love."

I smiled, nodding acknowledgement of her wise words, but I was still troubled.

Sirah looked at me closely, perceptive of my dark mood.

I told her openly, "You realize this is not the end of the war, it is only the beginning. It was just one battle. The Zarans will be back, and more numerous than ever. They will be out for bloody revenge worse than ever, but we will meet them sword for sword."

Sirah hugged me tightly and added, "My love, let us enjoy our victory today, there is plenty of time tomorrow and afterwards to do what must be done."

I nodded and lifted Sirah in my arms, bringing her lips to my own as I smothered her with gentle kisses.

CHAPTER 13

EMPEROR

That night a great victory celebration was held throughout the newly liberated city of Caliat. Tens of thousands of green men and women who had begun that day as slaves were now free men and women by nightfall. It was an exhilarating feeling for all.

Meanwhile, it appeared that not one Zaran winged man remained alive within the city, all of the enemy having been tracked down and put to the sword, with perhaps some few having escaped to one of their remaining stronghold cities.

Throughout the Great Hall of Caliat all the leaders who had been instrumental in the taking of the city were in attendance and celebrating our victory. There was speech making, drinking, heated talk, more drinking, shouting, still more drinking, the reliving of battles won, and the sad remembering of the brave dead. It was a somber but festive occasion for there was much for all of us to celebrate.

All of the leaders of the revolt were there except for Tar-Gool, who had done such a big part in making this day possible. He was the man most responsible for freeing his people from the oppression of the winged monsters who had terrorized them for so long.

Everyone throughout that massive royal hall was in attendance in rampant and wild celebration: Sahn Jor of the Woodworker Caste; Zaor, the new King of the Warrior Caste, along with his warrior clan chiefs Saok and Andu. Coron and Tavan representing the Southern Farmers were there drinking and carousing, as was Armen, king of the notorious Sar Nomads. He sat with his new friend and comrade, Ogz, the king of the fierce Vaki Nomads. It was amazing to see those two sitting together as comrades in arms and drinking as friends.

Zaor suddenly stood up and getting the attention of all the feasters, made a speech about what was to come in the war of the green people against the Winged-men. Then he ended his words by saying, "We have each pledged to wage a war to the death—to destroy the Zaran Winged-men and rid our world of these invaders forever!"

There was a mighty cheer that rang throughout the palace and eventually throughout the city, for all of the green-skinned peoples were now united to seek freedom from those of Zar.

When the cheers had died down, Zaor continued, getting more serious. "There are two items that I need to put forward at this time to you, my friends and fellow comrades. First is that I propose the city of Caliat be renamed in honor of one who is no longer with us and who was slain in the cause of seeking our freedom. Tar-Gool proved to be a great patriot and friend to freedom. I propose that we rename Caliat in his honor, and that from here on this city be known as Tarcos."

The entire hall reverberated with enthusiastic acclaim and cheers at this proposal. There was not one dissenting voice to be herd, so that the proposal was passed unanimously.

Zaor told all, "My friends, it is settled, from this moment on, Caliat will become the free city of Tarcos—and it will be the capital city of a new empire of our green-skinned race!"

There were great cheers of approval and shouts of joy to that.

When everyone settled down a bit, Zaor continued, "Now comrades and brothers in arms, one other item is necessary to be addressed by us all. It is rather a simple matter. We have a new empire! Well, we need an emperor for that empire! He must be a great warrior and a proven leader, proven in our war against the Zarans and instrumental in the fall of Caliat. He must be one man who all green peoples and all tribes and clans in our alliance respect and can agree upon. I think you all know that there is only one man on this world who can fit this bill. Had Tar-Gool lived, he no doubt, would have made a fine first emperor. However, Tar-Gool is no longer with us, and yet we are privileged to have one other among us, one who we all know and admire. This warrior has played a part of equal importance besides Tar-Gool in the defeat of the Zarans here today. I hereby call upon Jon Kirk to heed the call of his people, and accept the mantle of great responsibility and challenge to become first emperor of the new Green Empire of Ares!"

I was stunned by Zaor's words, they were totally unexpected, and I hardly knew what to say.

To my great surprise everyone in that huge chamber was even more enthusiastic for this proposal than they had been for Zaor's earlier one of changing the name of Caliat to Tarcos. Everywhere warriors wildly and proudly shouted their agreement, calling out for me to take the throne and become emperor.

I hardly knew what to say. Ares is a feudal world and the custom is to have clans and tribes, that sometimes join into states run by kings and emperors as rulers. That was their custom, but it was not mine. But was I not on Ares now? So should I not do as the native peoples did here? And more importantly, with my future mate Sirah, was I not becoming a Aresan too?

My heart swelled with pride and joy when I saw that all my lieutenants lead by Zaor, and accompanied by Armen, Sahn Jor, Ogz, and Tavan each came to stand before me. They stood before me with swords drawn and bowed to me in a salute of respect that almost brought tears to my eyes.

"Zaor?" I asked softly. "Armen, Sahn Jor…"

They all looked toward me with swords drawn in respect and chanted together, "All hail, Jon Kirk, Emperor of Ares!"

I did not know what to do or say just then. I was not emperor material. Oh, the easy thing would have been to accept the honor, but I wondered, was it really the right thing to do? I said nothing, thinking it through carefully. I looked at Sirah, and she smiled at me with her eyes full of love, then she nodded her assent. I took a deep breath and felt a great responsibility alight upon my shoulders. These were my people now and I was one of them.

Zaor told me in a soft voice, "You must accept the imperial throne, Jon Kirk. There is no other who can unite us. We need you."

I had heard his words but I sat still and silent. Thoughtful. It was the most important decision I would ever make in my life. I approached it seriously, for I knew that it was a great honor they were bestowing upon me, but that it would also mean incredibly hard work and massive responsibility. It would also take me away from my beloved Sirah, which was something that I did not want to happen ever again now that I had her here with me. We were together finally, but I knew we would have to part if I took the throne. We were at war. There was much work to do. It was a difficult decision. However Zaor's words came back to me, "We need you," he had told me. And that call to duty is something that I have never been able to turn my back upon. I was a soldier. I could not be selfish and keep to my own happiness with Sirah when the people of this world needed me. Duty is the constant credo of the fighting man, and it can not be denied.

Soon the noise and chanting, shouts and cries began in an ever growing crescendo, all there begging me to take the imperial throne. They chanted so loud I could swear that I saw the very walls of the palace shaking. Still I hesitated. I really did not want to accept this great honor or to have this incredible responsibility thrust upon me. I knew what it would mean. It was almost too much for any one man to bare, but I had a duty and a responsibility to lead as well. These people would need someone good to lead them, but also someone who could hold them together in the war that was on the way. It would be a most brutal war and it was coming soon. No mistake about that. The Zaran military would never allow the sack of Caliat to stand while there was one winged man left alive on this world to oppose it.

"Why do you hesitate?" Zaor asked me carefully.

"I do not know if I am worthy," I told my friend.

Zaor smiled, "Jon Kirk, the very fact that you seriously consider the question of your worthiness means that you are the correct choice. We need a strong leader, we need a good man who can unite us, keep us united and lead us to victory. You are that man, Jon Kirk. My Emperor!"

Armen added, "If you do not take the imperial throne all we have fought for here will come to nothing. All those who have died this day will have died for nothing. For the Zarans will be victorious over us without you to lead us. Your people need you, Jon Kirk. Heed their call. Lead us, my Emperor!"

The cheering still had not diminished, but seemed to be growing louder and more demanding. Even frantic now.

Zaor stood before me, motioned for the crowd to be silent, and when the ruckus died down a bit and all eyes were on him and I, he said to me directly in a loud voice that reverberated throughout that great hall, "Jon Kirk, will you take the throne and become Emperor?"

I stood up, tall, looked towards Sirah and saw the glow of a smile upon her face, then I walked towards Zaor and answered him in a loud voice that could be heard throughout that great hall, "Yes, I, Jon Kirk, accept the throne and the title of Emperor. You all do me a great honor and I shall do my best to live up to it!"

Well, at that point the entire hall erupted in hysterical shouts of sheer joy and approval, and soon the cheers and raucous cries spread throughout the city of Tarcos. There was immediate dancing and feasting through the streets of the city with much laughter and happiness.

Sirah came over to me then and kissed me sweetly.

"I hope I made the right decision," I told her in a quiet voice.

"Jon Kirk, my emperor," she said softly, holding me tightly. "I love you."

"And I you, Sirah," I said, bringing her close to me. I held her as if it was to be our one last happy time together. For I knew one dire fact, no one can know what the future holds.

* * * *

The feasting and dancing went on all night long. The city of Tarcos was going wild with joyous celebration that filled every street and every house. The people were free. There was hope again now for the men and women of Tarcos, freedom and hope. It was a heady brew when mixed with our recent victory over the Winged-men and lubricated with strong Ares wine and beer.

That night Sirah and I slept in separate quarters, for as yet we had had not time for any formal marriage, nor mating ceremony, as the Aresans call it. I was told that it would be unseemly for the emperor to share quarters with a women who was not his wife. I was already beginning to have second thoughts about taking this emperor job. But I respected their customs. They had become mine now, after all. Marriage was a very serious and sacred affair to the people of Ares, and not to be taken lightly. Sirah wanted our ceremony according to strict custom back in her village in the Coastal Mountains. Of course, I agreed. So we waited. I had waited for a woman like Sirah all my life, so a few more days did not make much difference in our love.

In the meantime, before that happy day would be upon us, I had the job of an emperor to perform. Tarcos had to be rebuilt and organized, the fortifications against the Winged-men were now drastically deficient. They had to be rebuilt. Watch towers had to be set up and scouts sent out to warn of any attack. I knew that we had to make Tarcos impregnable to attack by land and air. An attack which would surely come against us soon.

The main objective now however was to gather my lieutenants and have them form up what would become the new Ares Imperial Army. They had to find every able bodied green man who could fight and get them into the army, train them, and get them set for the battle that was coming. It was a massive undertaking. We also sent out scouts to gather fighters from all the clans and tribes throughout Ares. I wanted an army that would be big enough and trained to destroy the Winged-men. I did my best to seek out any who would aid us in freeing our world of the winged menace forever.

* * * *

The next day I awoke early, as is my usual custom, while most of those in the city still slept in deep and peaceful slumber. I could not sleep. I had severe responsibilities now that I took seriously and weighed heavily upon me. People would die if I made mistakes. I decided to check the guard posts, see what those few awake were doing. I was annoyed to discover that it seemed that guards had not been posted at all, but it was not entirely unexpected considering the previous night's activities and celebrations. Nevertheless, it distressed me to see the security so lax, even though I had ordered guards posted throughout the city on night and day schedules. This lack of security concerned me greatly.

As I took inventory of my surroundings that morning in the dead silence of the quiet palace, I was startled to see sinister shadows moving behind the tapestry at the windows of a corridor. I noticed that one of the large windows in my room had been left open, and I jumped with surprise when I finally saw a dozen Winged-men quietly entering my chamber. They had drawn swords and came in silently and most carefully.

I jumped up, drew my own sword and then charged them in a mad head-long attack. They were as surprised to see me as I was to see them. What were they doing here? Up to no good, for sure! I was on them fast and hard and had dropped three of their number right away. I thought I had them then, but my heart sank when from another window I noted more Winged-men entering the palace. And behind these invaders, I was shocked to see four bearded mountain warriors, who I instantly recognized as followers of the outlawed former king, Tob.

Then my eyes turned to hard cold diamonds, for I saw Tob himself! He was entering through the window at the other end of my chamber and was actually giving orders to the Winged-men, pointing at me and telling them, "Hurry, that is him! The one they call, Jon Kirk! Kill him quickly!"

CHAPTER 14

KING TOB RETURNS

Tob was back! The treacherous *chavas* was here now in my very own chamber in my own palace, and he had come with a group of Winged-men to carry out his plan to apparently assassinate me!

I grew red with rage and came at him and his men with death on the point of my blade and murder in my heart.

The battle became quite noisy with the incessant clang of metal blades and the curses and howls of pain from the wounds I inflicted on the enemy. The Winged-men who were fighting with Tob and his men did their best to get around my guard. They had a hard time. It galled me with after all we had been through I now saw green men and Winged-men fighting side by side against our green warriors. How could this happen? Now they were trying to cut me off, and then cut me down. But it was not to be. I fought them furiously, seeking shelter in a small alcove where they could only come at me one at a time. I immediately sounded the alarm and in bare moments the entire palace was alerted and seeking to repel the attackers.

Guards and warriors streamed into my suite of rooms and the outer corridors looking for the enemy. I saw Zaor enter my chamber at a run, sword in his hand ready for action. He immediately found the enemy and dispatched one of the winged intruders. Upon seeing Tob at the other end of the chamber he blurted out a curse and flew at the giant with extended sword in a fit of furious battle rage. He was a terrifying sight to behold and I knew he would offer me fierce competition for which one of us would get the pleasure of putting a sword through Tob's treacherous heart.

Tob, realizing all was lost now and that his secret attack was found out, left his men alone, seeking to escape from the same window that he had used to enter my chamber. He accomplished his retreat by being carried by a large winged man who flew away to safety with him upon his back. He was gone in a heartbeat.

Soon the fighting was over, for with Tob gone, those who remained were easy work for me and my men. The Winged-men who remained were cut down and Tob's treasonous green companions were put to the sword. Soon they were all dead, but Tob had once again escaped me.

"This is bad for us, Jon Kirk," Sahn Jor told me, wiping the blood from his blade now that the fighting was over and done with for the moment. "This Tob is a real troublemaker, by him bringing Winged-men and green men together to fight against us he has done something so low I never believed it would be possible. What a treacherous beast!"

I nodded, Sahn Jor didn't have to tell me about Tob, and I could not express my anger just then about Tob and what he had done.

Armen spit upon the floor to accentuate his own disgust with the treacherous creature named Tob.

I watched from my window as some fifty Winged-men flew away northward to safety with Tob among them. In their arms they carried Tob and some others of his own green warriors. I cringed when I noticed that among them was Crooch and Vakon, two even more treacherous cowards and traitors. It seemed all our enemies were uniting against us. I wondered what such a large force had been doing here because it did not seem that all of those winged fiends had been with Tob's group, and I had not seen Crooch or Vakon at all. I began to wonder if there had been a second group of invaders that had come here this night led by Crooch and Vakon. If so, just what had they been up to?

I remember thinking these dark thoughts as I watched my enemy fly away and how strange it all seemed to me that Tob had so many men still left alive, for surely we had cut down most of them. And then I realized the horrible truth, Tob had not just sent a force of fighters to my chamber, he had sent men to other chambers of the palace as well!

Then my heart hit the floor when I made out a slim female form in the clutches of one of the Winged-men flying away in the far off distance. I had assumed it had been just another of Tob's men, but upon a closer look I realized the truth.

It was Sirah!

My beloved was their captive!

Zaor had noticed that she was a captive now as well, and in silence he placed a comforting hand upon my shoulder.

"I am sorry, Jon Kirk," he said softly.

I was too shocked to reply.

"They will be going to the Coastal Mountains, I am sure," Zaor told me. "Manalia found out that Tob has taken over some of the highland tribes there. He hides there in exile. They are giving him aid and protection."

I shook my head in utter frustration hinged with terrible fear for my poor Sirah. And guilt that I had listened to custom and not keep myself in her room, that I had not protected her as I should have done. I had let her down and now she was lost to me.

"How is it that Winged-men fight with Tob?" Saok asked, not liking what he had seen here this night and seeking some explanation.

"I saw Crooch and Vakon in that pack of fiends also," I said in anger.

Zaor nodded, "Tob probably promised them the death of Jon Kirk and the fall of this city by your murder."

"He made a deadly mistake then," I growled, thinking of my beloved Sirah in his clutches. "He will be made to pay dearly for what he has done here this night! They all shall pay!"

* * * *

We learned later that Tob had made a promise to the winged monsters in exchange for their assistance. For the Zarans figured that with me dead, the alliance of green tribes and clans that had united against them would certainly fall apart. They might have been correct in their assumption, but they had failed. Now I was more determined than ever to rid this planet of the winged creatures who were not native to this planet and did not belong here. They were invaders and I would send them back to where they came from, or down into the Afterworld where they belonged. But first I would rescue Sirah and deal with Tob!

I was certain that Tob must have some more dastardly scheme in mind than merely killing me. He had also come for Sirah. I knew that was to force her to become his mate. I cringed at the thought, my anger boiling blood red. I would find Tob and avenge Sirah if it was the last thing that I did. I just hoped I had time enough to save her.

I saw to it immediately that preparations were made for me to leave Tarcos with a small force. We gathered our mounts, the fleet-footed Ares horse-like *pourk*, and my newly created imperial bodyguard, the Black Dragons, then left Tarcos and raced towards the Coastal Mountains.

The *pourk* is a large reptilian-like animal that is used on this world in much the same manner as a horse is used on Erath. In fact, green people of all regions of Ares pride themselves upon their great cavalries and the swift speed of these creatures. They came in useful now as I left Tarcos with a sufficient force to rescue Sirah and put an end to Tob once and for all. My Black Dragons were the best of the best.

Our journey was long and arduous, an uneventful two day race at a breakneck pace over the dead sea bottoms of Ares towards the faraway Coastal Mountains.

Scouts reported back to us that Tob's tribe lay hidden in the higher reaches of the mountains. It was a rough desolate region, rife with many fine places for ambush. We would have to enter with care. I was told that he had almost a thousand warriors under his command, though not all of them were with him now. Meanwhile I had a formidable cavalry force of one thousand of my brave mounted fighters fired up for revenge and battle. I was not only their leader, their emperor, but I was their most vocal advocate.

I had left Sahn Jor behind as military commander of Tarcos, along with fifty thousand warriors to defend the city in case of Zaran attack while I was gone. Meanwhile Zaor, Tavan, Coron, Andu, Armen and Ogz and many of their own troops rode with me.

After two tense days we came to Tob's village. It was, as I had expected, deserted. Tob was not so foolish to remain there knowing that my having survived his murder attempts I would be hard upon his heels for revenge. Upon examination of the village huts and caves we discovered many dead Winged-men and green male bodies that had been concealed in the caves. I wondered what had happened here.

Ogz pointed at the dead, said, "See, Jon Kirk, even a treacherous *chavas* such as Tob can not trust a Zaran. I think these men where killed by their winged allies once their usefulness was over?"

"Yes, it appears they fell upon each other," Armen spoke up, examining the bodies carefully. "I think I might know where Tob may be, Jon Kirk."

I looked over at Armen and asked, "Where?

Armen smiled, then said, "I believe that he is in the last place that we would ever look for him."

"What do you mean?" I asked, my temper growing short. Then I looked at Armen and gasped, "You mean…?"

"Yes, Jon Kirk, Tob is probably on his way back to Tarcos even as we speak."

I looked carefully at my companion and friend. I shook my head, his words did not make sense to me, but then our scouts came in and reported there was no sign of Tob or his men in the mountains. No word had come back to us of his presence there.

Iruk, one of the Vaki Nomad scouts told me, "All signs point to Tob having left the mountains, Jon Kirk."

I nodded, feeling a desperate doom clouding my thoughts. A double-crosser like Tob might double back to the scene of his crime. It seemed probable. But why? I knew that most of the tribes here would not support him, but he was an ardent coward who would seek the most help he could from whatever source he could find. Perhaps Tob had some treacherous plan of his own using his winged allies to get him into the city? But, then again, why? Perhaps to open the gates to allow the enemy hosts to enter unawares? Perhaps he had stolen Sirah knowing that I would mount a rescue for her, and being led away from the city, Tarcos would be vulnerable to attack? Perhaps Tob even knew of some secret entrance, either told to him by his winged allies or by those lying dogs Crooch and Vakon? They had to be involved in some way. Whatever it was, they were all up to no good.

These dark thoughts swirled within my mind as Zaor advanced to me with an old man at his side. I had to decide, and quickly.

"This man is a lone survivor, Jon Kirk, and he told me the story of having seen Tob's band double back in mad flight toward Tarcos."

"The man's words are reliable?" I asked Zaor.

"I would stake my life on it, My Emperor."

I nodded, well, that did it. If I had not made up my mind before, that surely did it.

"Quickly, we ride back to Tarcos. There is treachery afoot. I was lead out here so I would be away from the city. That means Tarcos is in danger!"

"A secret attack?" Armen asked.

"Maybe, my friend, but let us get back before it is too late," I ordered grimly.

It wasn't long before one of my most trusted agents, Kali, reported back to me with the news that he had spotted Tob's band. This man was unique in my force, for he used a captive Zaran winged man as his mount, forcing the beast under his control to fly him in the air to gather intelligence over vast distances. His reports were vital.

Kali told me, "Tob has about a hundred men with him, and your Lady Sirah is still held captive. They are mounted now on *pourks*, not being flown by the winged demons, and are riding steady due south."

I thanked Kali, then talked with my officers about what I should do. Armen had a plan to cut Tob's force off from the city and trap them. He knew of a passage through the mountains, a short cut we could take.

It did not take us long to catch up with Tob's band and trap them. When we came upon them there was a short battle, bloody and quick, and then it was over. Within the hour I had Sirah free and back in my arms again where she belonged.

Unfortunately, Tob, Crooch and Vakon, along with a handful of their men escaped once again and fled eastward into Zaran lands.

"This Tob is a wily creature," Coron observed.

"And Crooch and Vakon are his equal in treachery," Zaor added in anger that all had eluded us once again. "They make quite the treacherous trio."

I savored holding Sirah in my arms. At least she was safe, and that was the most important thing for me now, far above catching that trio of poisonous snakes. There would be time enough for them some day. With that in mind I sent Armen and Zaor with two forces of a hundred fighters each to hunt down Tob and his band of men and bring them back to me. Alive, if possible. I had plans for Tob. And for Crooch and Vakon as well.

THE WINGED MEN | 129

In the meantime, Sirah and I were reunited and happy once again at being in each other's arms and would soon return to Tarcos under the protection of my Black Dragons. But first there was one more thing to do.

"I'll never leave you alone again!" I told Sirah firmly.

"Never, Jon Kirk," she said kissing me furiously. "I thought I would never see you again."

"And I you, my beloved."

"Well, we are together now, my love."

"Yes, now and for always," I told her.

That night I lost no time in making Sirah my lawful wife as per Ares custom. We rode quickly to Sirah's village in the eastern Coastal Mountains. There were not many of the village men there because so many of them had been stationed in posts within Tarcos. However, the women and children were everywhere, and all came out to welcome Sirah and I, along with our escort. That evening, in a simple but elegant ceremony, Sirah and I were bonded as one, mated according to Ares custom. It was a splendid ceremony, topped off by a massive feast. Finally Sirah and I were husband and wife. It was a joyous occasion for us and the happiest day of our lives.

That night we feasted and sang war songs and danced sacred dances. Sirah and I slept out in the crisp mountain air and made love with a million stars shining down upon us until the fire-red Ares sun proclaimed the dawn of a new day. It was glorious.

CHAPTER 15

THE END OF THE BEGINNING

Two days later Zaor and Armen returned with their warriors to the village where we were waiting for them to meet up. They did not have good news for us. They had been unable to overtake Tob's lead, nor take down Crooch or Vakon, for they had been attacked by a large Winged-men force from the Zaran city of Scresa. For now, the treacherous trio as we called them, would have to be forgotten as more pressing matters needed to be dealt with. The Winged-men from the other cities were planning their attack against us.

In the meantime, I and my new wife were introduced for the first time to my friends as Emperor Jon Kirk and Lady Sirah to resounding cheers and good fellowship. Then another round of congratulations and feasting was held for my friends and fighters.

Zaor was overjoyed, "Jon Kirk, it is about time the two of you joined as one!"

I smiled, hugged Sirah tightly and nodded towards my friend, "Lady Sirah has a most wise brother. He is also a good friend. Thank you."

* * * *

The next morning we all left for Tarcos. On the way there we decided to gather together all the people of Sirah and Zaor's village, along with many members of the mountain tribes, all their warriors, women, and children. They were joined by Sahn Jor's woodworkers and more tribes and clans who were seeking security and shelter in Tarcos, the capital city of the new Green Empire of Ares which I now ruled.

Warriors, hunters, woodworkers, miners, metal workers and all other castes and clans from throughout the planet had been evacuated from the mountains and their places of hiding for so long.

They were exiles on their own world no longer. We took with us entire tribes, entire villages, as well as many of their possessions in what would go down in history as the Great Trek to Tarcos. The coming home of the green people of Ares. It was a massive exodus, and though constantly harassed by small bands of Winged-men, we were too large a group to attack effectively. We made good time and reached Tarcos in just six days.

What we saw when we reached Tarcos was a former run-down city that had long been under occupation of the lazy and useless Zarans, seemingly instantly transformed into a bustling and glorious capital of a new vibrant empire that shone with hope and promise. It had been weeks since the old city of Caliat had fallen. In that time Tarcos had been at peace, and no Winged-men dared even venture near it.

I noticed added fortifications and redoubts that had been built up all around the city walls. Outposts and scouts were constantly scanning the skies and surrounding plains for any signs of the enemy by land or air.

"Sahn Jor has done well here," I told Zaor as we entered the city in a long procession to the wild cheers of the people. It was good to see the people—my people—so happy and our procession soon became a victory parade.

"The people of this city have hope and vitality again," Zaor replied. "It is a good thing to see, Jon Kirk."

By this time many of the delegates we had sent to all other villages and caste groups throughout Ares were now sending us their promises of support. There were many people who had been in exile during the long harsh years of Zaran rule. Now they all came to join our cause. It was not long before we received messages from castes and tribes on the other side of the continent, from the Cattle Herding Castes, the Northern Farmers, and even the Ag Nomads. The metalworker Caste and the Miners promised to send fighting men, but they also told us they world mine the metal and turn it into good swords for our men to use in battle. This was also most welcome.

There was also good news on another front. Our victory had sown the seeds of unrest throughout the other five Zaran cities and now those seeds had borne fruit with revolts breaking out in most of those centers of the enemy. In all areas of Ares under Zaran control there was turmoil and rebellion brewing among the enslaved green peoples. The Winged-men's own cities were experiencing unrest and sabotage. And while this unrest was often quickly and brutally put down by Zaran troops, it did not end, but would always spring up again elsewhere no sooner did the Zaran troops leave. I knew what had to be done now, I had to gather our army to help these people, spur a revolt of the green peoples throughout the planet, then sack and destroy every one of those five Zaran cities and put every last Winged-men to the sword.

CHAPTER 16

ATTACKED BY THE ZARANS

It was not long before my expeditionary force of fighters was ready, my vaulted Black Dragons in their lead.

As before I tasked Sahn Jor with the job of staying behind with a third of our troops to defend Tarcos if there should be any attack on the city. Then with Zaor, Armen, and the remainder of my army, now over a hundred thousand fighters, we rode to aid our allies in the other Zaran cities in the north and west. I now considered these cities part of our empire and merely occupied by the Zarans. They were no longer Zaran cities at all any longer. They belonged to the people of Ares, the true people of this world, the green people. Soon I knew we would free our people from the Winged-men forever!

My mighty force of fighters were now ready to leave Tarcos when reports began to come in of a huge army of Winged-men advancing upon the city. There were winged flyers out front of the approaching horde as scouts, but there was a larger ground contingent, including massive cavalry, wagons, mighty siege engines and flying warriors now armed with spears and arrows. It was a deadly assemblage.

I looked like an impressive and dangerous force. It was obvious the Zarans were planning to try and crush us in one massive blow. I however, was not impressed.

"Well then, we can not leave now," I said ordering a change in plans. "I feared this day would come. We must defend the city."

"How many of them are there?" Zaor asked me curiously.

"Reports from our scouts say as many as half a million!" Coron said with concern.

I whistled in awe, smiling at my officers.

"Well we are certainly outnumbered, maybe by five to one. But what else is new? We are always outnumbered and we always win!' Armen said returning my smile. He was itching for a fight against the Zarans, and so were every one of my officers.

Zaor looked at me and said, "We have stood up against worse odds, eh, Jon Kirk, my emperor?"

I nodded, looking at Armen and Zaor, putting my hand on Sahn Jor's shoulder, and told them all, "I feel very confident in spite of the fact we are outnumbered, my friends. With men like you at my side, they can never win against us."

CHAPTER 17

THE END OF JON KIRK'S TRANSMISSION

Suddenly the vision of Jon Kirk—where his image had been sitting before me in my living room back on Earth telling me his strange story—began to slowly fade out. One moment Jon Kirk was there, the next minute he was gone!

"What happened? Jon Kirk, where are you?" I shouted.

I found myself suddenly alone.

What had happened? I was shocked and did not know what to make of this strange turn of events. Then, just as suddenly as he had disappeared, Jon Kirk mysteriously reappeared.

"You are back!" I shouted greatly relieved. He was there with me once again as before, standing in front of me now, in the living room of my house back on Earth.

"I am sorry, my old friend," Jon Kirk told me with a grim smile. "This equipment is very old. It once belonged to Tar-Gool, and I am afraid it is not in very good working order."

"Where are you now?" I asked him, bursting with curiosity.

"In the old abandoned fortress of Tar-Gool," Jon Kirk replied to me thoughtfully. I sensed there was something he was holding back from telling me. I began to get a bad feeling, one of impending doom.

"What is it, Jon Kirk?" I asked trying to hold down my alarm. "Tell me what is wrong!"

He did not answer me immediately, for he looked forlorn, sad. What did it mean?

"Will you continue your story, Jon? What happened when the Zarans attacked your forces at the city of Tarcos?" I asked fascinated, seeking more answers to his strange tale.

"Yes, I will continue, if you want me to do so."

"Of course I want you to continue," I pleaded now, enthusiastic. "What happened when you saw the Zaran army approach your city?"

Jon Kirk allowed a slim smile and told me, "Well, the Zarans had gathered a massive host of almost half a million fighters. We were outnumbered in Tarcos by five to one. It was not long before the enemy had our city surrounded. Their plan was to starve us out. Tarcos soon lay under siege, and the Winged-men had us completely cut off."

Once again the image of Jon Kirk began to flicker and fade. Then he disappeared altogether.

Jon Kirk was gone!

I waited, hoped, prayed for his return.

I sat there alone in my living room the rest of the night, but Jon Kirk never reappeared. I wondered what had happened to him. Had some winged assassin's blade found his noble heart? Had Tob finally been able to kill my friend? Or maybe it was some action by wily Crooch or vile Vakon? Those two were always up to no good. Or perhaps it was just that silly old transmitter of Tar-Gool's that had gone one the whack again?

Since that evening of June 21st, a full year has passed and I have not heard from my friend, Jon Kirk. That feeling of impending doom that I had felt surrounding him and the green people of Tarcos when I had last seen him was still with me. Had Tarcos finally been taken by the Zarans? Was Tob up to some new treachery? What of Sirah?

I thought about Jon Kirk and his lovely Lady Sirah all that long year. I thought about his friends and comrades in arms, Zaor, Armen, Sahn Jor, and all the others who fought bravely at his side and for the cause of Ares freedom.

How did Jon Kirk's strange story end?

Perhaps I was never to know.

* * * *

It has now been sixteen months since Jon Kirk had first told me his strange story that warm summer day in June. Now it was dark and cold in the middle of winter, and I had almost completely given up hope of ever hearing from him again.

Then I received a letter from a friend that told me he had seen Jon Kirk in New York, and that Jon had told him that he had a manuscript that would be sent to me at a later date. He told me that it would be the second volume of Jon Kirk's incredible adventures upon the planet Ares.

Now I check the mail box every day, but to date no such package as been delivered to me. But I am ever hopeful. If Jon Kirk says he will do something, then he will surely do it. So I wait. Patiently. After all, I know my old friend has more important matters to attend to as the emperor of his own world and the leader of a war for freedom.

So I will wait.

I know it will be something worth waiting for!